WHEN LIFE GIVES YOU LEMONS, MAKE PEACH PIE

THE GREAT PEACH EXPERIMENT

WHEN LIFE GIVES YOU LEMONS, MAKE PEACH PIE

ERIN SODERBERG DOWNING

PIXEL✚INK

For my incredible kids,
who are always up for adventure

PIXEL✚INK

Text copyright © 2021 by Erin Soderberg Downing
All rights reserved. Pixel+Ink is a division of TGM Development Corp.

Printed and bound in February 2021 at Maple Press, York, PA, U.S.A.

Book design and interior illustrations by Michelle Cunningham
Freddy's artwork by Henry Downing

www.pixelandinkbooks.com

First Edition
Library of Congress Control Number: 2020940463
Hardcover ISBN 978-1-64595-034-9
eBook ISBN 978-1-64595-060-8

1 3 5 7 9 10 8 6 4 2

Erin Soderberg Downing is a fiscal year 2020 recipient of an Artist Initiative
grant from the Minnesota State Arts Board. This activity is made possible
by the voters of Minnesota through a grant from the Minnesota State
Arts Board, thanks to a legislative appropriation by the Minnesota State
Legislature; and by a grant from the National Endowment for the Arts.

1

THE PROBLEM WITH PEACHES

Lucy Peach needed a new last name. *Peach* just wasn't working for her anymore. The problem with peaches, she'd come to realize, is they were too soft. Often, the sweet, fuzzy fruit appeared perfect on the outside—but when you bit into one, it surprised you with a mouthful of mushed-up mess. Lucy *Watermelon* would be a better fit, perhaps. Watermelons were tougher.

Twelve-year-old Lucy was busy pondering this and other important matters—such as which book she would dive into first on Saturday, the first day of summer break—when she heard a clank and a screech, followed by a whole lot of noisy clatter. The sound had come from somewhere outside.

Most of the time, noises like this could be attributed to one of Lucy's two younger brothers. Ten-year-old

Freddy loved creating enormous art projects, which often resulted in very messy—and sometimes *loud*—disasters. But with a sound like this, Lucy would put her money on the youngest Peach: Herb. Over the past few years, eight-year-old Herb had built up a huge pile of *stuff* in the garage. Lucy had warned him time and again that it was just a matter of time before it toppled over. She had a sinking suspicion today was that day.

Lucy crawled out of the pillow-stuffed reading fort she'd set up inside her bedroom closet and raced outside to fix whatever disaster needed fixing. Ever since their mom had died nearly two years before, this was Lucy's responsibility: she was the fixer. That's why *Peach* simply didn't cut it anymore. . . . It was Lucy's job to be tough, with a thick skin.

Outside, she was surprised to find both Freddy and Herb standing at the edge of the family's postage stamp–sized front lawn. She joined her brothers, and all three kids stared in wonder as a massive, bright orange truck backed up their slim driveway. The truck had knocked over the family's recycling bin, and cans and bottles were scattered everywhere. That, Lucy realized, explained the clatter.

Their dad, Walter, stood waiting at the foot of the driveway, rubbing his hands together like the slightly mad scientist he was. "Isn't she a beauty?" Dad asked, waving his arm toward the giant beast of a truck.

"A beauty!" Herb echoed.

"What *is* it?" Lucy asked, reaching down to start gathering up the spilled recycling. She neatly piled the cans and bottles on the lawn, to get them out of the way until she could return them to the bin.

"It's a food truck," Dad said, as if that explained everything.

"Are we throwing a party?" Freddy asked, his eyes wide with excitement. Then, as always, Lucy's middle brother couldn't resist sharing a few random fun facts. "You can hire a food truck to cater pretty much any kind of event. I saw a show about food trucks, and there's one that makes cotton candy on the spot. There's also a truck that serves food made out of meat that would otherwise go to waste—like pigeons and animal feet and other nasty stuff like that. Oh! And there's another one that sells *fugu*!"

"What's fugu?" little Herb asked, as though that were the most pressing question at the moment.

"Puffer fish. If it's not prepared correctly, you can die from eating it," Freddy informed him.

Dad chuckled. "Very interesting, Freddy. But no, we're not having a party. And we're definitely not eating fugu."

"Dad," Lucy said seriously, "*why* is there a food truck in our driveway?"

Walter Peach put on a wobbly smile and gestured to the giant vehicle. "She's all ours."

"This food truck . . . ," Lucy began, feeling a nervous lump form in her stomach, "is *ours?*"

"That's right," Dad said. "This summer, the Peaches are going to set out to explore the country!"

Lucy closed her eyes and drew in a sharp breath. "Oh, Dad," she said. Their father had done a lot of strange, frustrating, and irresponsible things over the past few years. But this was a new level of crazy. Lucy asked, "In a . . . *food truck?* Why?"

"Traveling the country in a food truck was one of your mother's big dreams," Dad explained. "And an adventure like this will be a wonderful way to honor her memory."

"How are we supposed to pay for this?" she asked.

Dad gave Lucy a secretive smile. It was the kind of smile that made her more than a little worried. "I've been sitting on some big news," he said. "*Very* big news."

Next to Lucy, hopeful Herb wiggled in anticipation. Freddy rubbed his hands together. Lucy hated seeing her brothers get excited about things she knew were certain to fall apart.

"Kids, one of your mother's inventions has sold," Dad finally announced.

Lucy gawped at him. Before she died, their mom, Madeline, had worked as a chemist. She'd invented many things, but none of those things had ever amounted to much. Yet Mom had never seemed to worry about that. She always told her kids that what she loved most about her job was getting to nurture something from the seed of an idea to a finished product, even when the seed didn't grow quite how she'd expected it to. Their mom always took great joy in the *process* of creating something new, just like Freddy did with his art.

Dad cleared his throat. "Before she got sick, do you remember that your mom was developing solar window clings?"

Of *course* Lucy remembered. She and Freddy had helped Mom come up with that project! After reading an article about solar energy and wind farms, Lucy had asked her mom if there was anything regular people, like the Peaches, could use to catch energy. Then Freddy started going on and on about how *ugly* solar panels and windmills are and asked why no one ever painted them cool colors.

Just a few days later, Mom and her team started creating a special kind of solar cling that could be printed

with lots of fun colors and designs. Regular people could stick them to any window in their house, where they would capture solar power—helping collect energy from the sun—while also turning the window into a piece of art. Mom had even used some of Freddy's drawings on one of the designs! Though Herb had been too little to help much, he'd been the one who kept Mom company at the lab—hopping and babbling away in his bouncy chair—when she put in extra time at work on weekends.

Dad smiled proudly. "The solar clings were your mother's pièce de résistance, kids. Her lab sold the cling technology to a big company that is going to mass-produce them. Mom's share of the profits is one point three million dollars." Dad held his hands out wide. "Kids, in technical terms, we are millionaires."

2

THE PLAN

"Millionaires! We are *millionaires!*" Herb wrapped his arms around Lucy's waist and hugged her tight, screaming with joy.

"A million dollars?" Lucy gasped. Herb loosened his hug. "Are you sure?"

Herb glanced at his big brother, whose mouth was hanging open. Suddenly, Freddy shook his head and said, "Is someone going to deliver a giant check? Will a fancy limo pull up with briefcases full of cash? Can we ask for all the money in two-dollar bills or state quarters?"

"Can we *please* get a pool in our backyard?" Herb begged. "The kind with a slide, and a diving board, and—*ooh! ooh!*—maybe some live fish swimming in the shallow end?"

"Live fish in a pool?" Freddy said with a laugh. "The chlorine would leave you with a pool full of *dead* fish." His eyes widened, and he added, "Unless we got one of those *saltwater* pools, and we could get a pet shark—"

"Guys," Lucy said, holding up a hand. "Focus. There's a food truck parked in our driveway. Remember?"

"Can we use part of the money to go somewhere amazing?" Freddy asked, ignoring their big sister altogether. "I've always wanted to visit the Chihuly glass museum in Seattle. While we're there, we could also check out Seattle's gum wall, which is this alley covered in millions of pieces of chewed-up gum!" He grinned and high-fived Herb. "It would also be fun to touch a pyramid, so we could see how they built those things. And wouldn't it be great if we could see some of the art in the National Gallery and check out the prison museum in London?" He bounced on his toes and added, "Hey, did you know you can walk inside catacombs filled with dead-guy skulls under the streets of Paris?"

"Now, kids, let's not get carried away," Dad said. "Those are all perfectly nice ideas, but I've got something even *more* special planned for this money. I think it's most appropriate for us to use a portion of your mom's windfall to live out one of her biggest dreams. That's why this summer, we'll be exploring the country and starting up our very own food truck business." Dad's voice caught as he swept his arm wide and pointed in the direction of Mrs. Halvorson's house at the end of their street. "Let's hit the highway and head out of Duluth. Take some time to live life on the road and reconnect as a family."

Before any of the kids could ask questions or respond, Dad barreled on. "We'll kick things off in just a few days, once summer break is officially underway. We can get our feet wet right here in Minnesota. Our first stop will take us a few hours south, to Minneapolis. Then we're going to head in a mighty loop, visiting Chicago, Ann Arbor, Columbus, Nashville; and if we're lucky, we'll even hit Indianapolis and majestic St. Louis."

In his mind, Herb pictured the illustrated map of the United States that hung on his second-grade classroom wall. He tried to remember where all those cities were, but couldn't. Tomorrow he'd spend read-aloud time studying the map. Maybe his teacher would even be willing to take a picture of it and print a copy for him!

Freddy closed his eyes and whispered, "Please tell me this food truck trip means I get to skip summer school?"

Herb couldn't understand why his brother was dreading summer school. Herb *loved* school. Personally, *he* didn't like summer vacation, because it meant saying goodbye—to his beautiful and wise second-grade teacher, his classmates, the class hamster he'd been in charge of feeding each day, his special cubby decorated with puffy stickers, and all the artwork his teacher had collected and carefully hung up throughout the year. Herb had responsibilities in Room 122. And he did not like to say goodbye. At least he had third grade to look forward to.

Dad nodded. "Yes, Freddy, I'm afraid you will likely miss most of summer school. But to make up for it, I ordered some math workbooks so you can practice over the summer." He looked from Herb to Freddy to Lucy. "So . . . ? What do you say? Good adventure, or *great* adventure? I think it's exactly how your mother would have wanted us to spend the money."

Herb clapped and gave Dad a big hug. "That *does* sound like a great adventure!"

"What about your wor—" Lucy began.

But before she could finish her sentence, a man stepped out of the food truck and thrust a clipboard at their dad. "I checked everything over and it all looks good. Sign here to confirm delivery," the guy said, "then I can be on my way."

While the adults took care of business, Herb crept

over to the massive vehicle and popped open the big door at the back. It creaked and groaned as it swung wide. He longed to climb up into the back of the truck to see what treasures were hidden inside, but he couldn't get his knee high enough to slide in. He hopped back down and covered his nose. "Pee-yew," he announced. The truck smelled a lot like their big plastic trash bin next to the garage on the day before the garbage collectors came.

"Mom sold a million-dollar invention and Dad bought a *used* food truck?" Lucy muttered. Herb thought his sister sounded annoyed. But then she gently wrapped her hands under Herb's armpits and boosted him up into the truck. He giggled and rolled aboard.

As soon as Herb was in, Freddy and Lucy hopped up. Standing in tallest-to-shortest order (and longest-to-shortest *hair* order)—Lucy, Freddy, then Herb—the Peach kids looked very much like an age progression of the same person: All had almost matching greenish brown speckled eyes that they'd gotten from their dad, and thick, messy brownish hair that they'd gotten from their mom. Except Herb, who had almost no hair at all (Freddy had helped him shave it all off after head lice took over his second-grade classroom for the fourth time that school year). Though the three kids looked alike, they could not have been more different. But Lucy always said their differences in personality helped make it easier for the three of them to get along.

Together, the Peach kids began to explore. The inside of the truck was grimy, and the air stale. It smelled awful, and Herb noticed some shriveled-up pieces of old, brown lettuce tucked into a few of the corners. There was also a mound of something orange-green and mysteriously smooshy-looking in the middle of one of the countertops. There were rags tossed about, and a half-full trash can inside a cabinet. How did this "look good," Herb wondered, remembering what the deliveryman had said.

The space was smaller than Herb would have expected. There was just a long, narrow passageway to walk through, and the rest of the truck's insides were filled with equipment. One side of the interior had a long metal counter, and underneath was a row of shiny cabinets that slid and swung open. Up above that counter were more shelves and storage areas. Toward the front of the truck was something that looked like a large, shiny oven with a whole bunch of different chambers. There were also several short refrigerators and freezers, a small stove and griddle thing, and even a sink. Herb quickly scanned the space, searching for the beds. Dad had said they would be traveling around the country in the food truck, and he couldn't figure out where they were going to sleep.

"I call this counter for my bed!" Herb cried out, eager to claim dibs on a prime spot before it was too late.

"We're not going to be *sleeping* in here, you neener," Freddy said, bonking him on the head with his hand.

"Then where *are* we sleeping?" Herb asked.

"Hotels, I assume," Lucy said. This announcement made Herb excited. Hotels had pools!

Just as Herb clambered up onto one of the counters to explore the shelves and cubbies higher up, Dad poked his head around the back door of the truck. "Well?" he prompted. Herb thought his dad looked a little nervous. "What do you think?"

"It needs a good scrubbing," Freddy said, his head buried deep inside one of the fridges. He pulled out a bag with a chunk of something that looked like moldy cheese.

"I think it's beautiful," Herb chimed in.

"The oven is almost new," Dad said proudly, pointing. "Isn't it great? I knew it must be a sign that I was on the right track when I found the perfect used truck for sale. This one was originally a custom-built truck for a family like ours—it has a special cab with two rows and four seatbelts up front, so we can all ride together, plus room underneath the cab for luggage. And everything is apparently in great working order. It's a pretty basic kitchen, but we'll make do."

"Wait . . . ," Lucy said. "You didn't spend a whole million bucks on this piece of junk, did you?" She was the most sensible of the Peach kids. In a very adult-sounding tone, she continued, "I seriously hope you set aside some of the money for other things, like charity and college and paying off debts and retirement savings."

"Y-yes," Dad said, stuttering slightly. "That's exactly right, Lucy. In fact, I donated a large portion of Mom's earnings to a cancer-research charity—that's certainly one thing she would have done if she were still alive. I also set a chunk aside to help with college for you kids, and our house payments." He sighed. "But I also thought Mom would like to see me use a small portion of the profits for fun. She was always encouraging me to take more risks and let loose a little. So, I put some of the money aside for us to use as a family—ten percent of what remained after taxes."

"Ten percent of $1.3 million is $130,000," Herb announced. They had been working on percentages in his special advanced math program that spring.

Lucy added, "So, assuming we need to save about forty percent of *that* for taxes, that means we have about seventy-five thousand bucks left over to use for fun stuff. Is that right?"

Dad nodded, looking delighted to see his kids' math skills hard at work. Lucy gingerly poked a piece of shriveled lettuce with the toe of her shoe and muttered, "Dad . . . do you actually think this trip is going to get off the ground? Or is this just another one of your big ideas that's going to fizzle in a few days?"

Herb's head swiveled from his sister to his dad, waiting for Dad's answer. Freddy, however, was nowhere to be seen. Herb had noticed that his brother often disappeared when they talked about Mom, or when Lucy and Dad started bickering.

In Lucy's defense, Dad *had* come up with lots of ideas that had gone all wrong over the past few years. But maybe that was because Mom had been the fun, adventurous one and, well . . . Dad was great, too, but in a different way. After Mom died, Dad had talked about planning family trips to some of Mom's favorite places—the Icehotel in Sweden, the Black Hills, Scotland, the Boundary Waters Canoe Area Wilderness—but they hadn't happened yet. Then there was the skydiving trip for four that Dad had paid for, in full, before he realized he was the only one old enough to actually jump out of a plane (and Dad was scared of heights)—so that idea had been a bust, too. Herb still got sad whenever he thought about the cat, Cream, they'd adopted before realizing Freddy was allergic.

Dad cleared his throat. Patches of bright pink

suddenly colored his pale cheeks. "Here's the thing," he began, his voice soft. "Many years ago, your mother and I used to plan for and dream about all of the nutty things we might someday do with our lives. When I was younger, I dreamed of writing short stories or dabbling in the arts. I took a sculpting class in college, you know?"

Freddy poked his head out from under the counter, where he'd been hiding. "*You* took an art class?"

"Indeed." Dad nodded. "But once we started grad school and teaching, and got wrapped up in our research," he said, running a shaking hand through his wispy hair, "there wasn't time for that kind of nonsense anymore. Your mom continued to talk about those someday dreams—her hope of eventually sailing around the world, and exploring hidden cities in Europe. She longed to open a small inn, where she could get to know adventurous travelers from near and far. In the year before she died, she talked often about how much she would love to run a food truck as a family." Dad propped his foot up on the truck's giant back bumper. "She thought it would be something fun we could do together. Mom loved that a food truck offered the best parts of so many adventures: a chance to meet new people, travel, and experience the thrill of building something from the ground up."

Herb wished he could remember his mom talking about this kind of stuff, but the truth was, he couldn't. Then, all of a sudden, he remembered playing with an old plastic food truck with his mom. They would set up tiny plastic food on the counters and use his collection of LEGO people as customers. They had called the game Restaurant, and sometimes Mom would hide real treats inside the food truck for Herb to find—chocolate chips, silver and gold Hershey's Kisses, a handwritten note wrapped around a piece of hard candy.

Dad's voice broke into Herb's memory. "Way back when, your mom put all her big ideas on hold so I could pursue my career," he said. "I always promised her we would do some of those crazy things later." He didn't say it, but even Herb knew they were all thinking the same thing: there had been no *later* for Mom.

"Getting all this money from one of Mom's big ideas . . . well, it feels like a sign," Dad said with a shrug. "It's like Mom is telling me it's time to go for it."

Herb didn't remember as much about their mom as Freddy or Lucy did. He had just turned six when she died. One of his favorite memories was from a regular day when she'd brought him to the park, just the two of them. He'd been nervous to go down the biggest slide;

it was tall and steep, and there was a mound of scratchy sand at the bottom of the plastic chute. But Mom had convinced him to try it. When he got all the way up to the top, he'd leaned down to see if she was watching. The wind was blowing her big, soft, fluffy hair all around, and Herb had giggled because it looked like a tumbleweed. She'd given him a thumbs-up and a big, confident smile, and said, "Go for it, Herbie." Herb liked the idea of this food truck being some kind of sign, and he liked thinking about his mom telling them to *go for it*. "Then let's go for it," he whispered. "It can be our very own family experiment, for Mom. She always loved experimenting."

Freddy crawled out from under the counter and crept closer to Dad, who was still standing alone outside the back door. "The Great Peach Experiment," Freddy added with a little smile. "For Mom." He nodded and whacked one of the counters with his fist. Then he got right down to business. "So, Dad . . . you're saying we're actually going to be *running* this food truck? What kind of food are we going to be selling?"

"Aha!" Dad hopped up to join the kids inside the truck. It suddenly felt quite squished with all four of them squeezed in together. And Dad had to stand slightly stooped; if he stretched up to his full height, his balding head scraped the ceiling. "I thought that could be our first order of business as a family. We need to pick a theme for our truck. Something catchy. And uniquely *Peach.*"

"You're telling me you bought a food truck and are planning to start up a business with it, but you don't know what *kind* of food we're selling? And this is a good idea *how?*" Lucy asked. Herb caught his sister rolling her eyes. She muttered, "Maybe we should sell peaches?"

"Or peaches-and-cream ice cream!" Herb hoped the idea of ice cream might cheer his sister up. "And other ice cream and malts and stuff? Mom liked ice cream." He closed his eyes, trying to remember her favorite flavor, but he couldn't.

Lucy grinned at him. "Do you guys remember, her favorite flavor was Superman?" she asked, as if she'd read Herb's mind. "Just like you, Herbie. Mom liked that it turned her tongue all kinds of funny colors."

Herb giggled. "I like that, too."

"And I like your spirit, Herb," Dad said. "An ice cream truck is a nice idea, but we have this fancy, nearly new, multichambered oven and a stove in the truck. Seems like we should use them somehow."

"Monster cookies!" Freddy suggested. "Or tacos. Maybe both! Everyone likes tacos and cookies."

"I *do* like cookies and tacos," Dad said. He scratched his bald spot, which was surrounded by fluffy puffs of blond hair. "Hmmm."

"Or . . . ," said Lucy, "maybe we should pick a food we already know how to make and go with that?"

Herb shrugged. "But what do we know how to make?" Most nights, Lucy made him and Freddy grilled cheese or omelets or butter noodles or smoothies or soup for dinner. They were all yummy, but none of those items seemed special enough for a food truck.

There was a long silence, during which Dad swung a cabinet door back and forth, back and forth. It squeaked and sighed, filling the silence. No one said anything. Finally, Dad blurted out: "What about Aunt Lucinda's wonderful peach pie? I haven't made it in years, but she did teach me how to make it. It was your mom's favorite." He furrowed his brow and added quietly, "At least, she always told *Lucinda* it was her favorite. . . ."

"Peach pie," Freddy said, smiling. "That's catchy."

"Catchy," echoed Herb.

Lucy shook her head, but then she muttered, "I guess it's settled, then."

"The Peach Pie Truck," Herb cheered. "Yum yum."

Just as Herb said that, the cabinet door Dad had been swinging back and forth popped off its hinges and clattered to the floor. In the silence that followed, Dad gave his kids a forced smile, and said, "This summer is going to be great!"

HOW TO SPEND A MILLION DOLLARS

When I have a million bucks of my own, I'm going to buy a limo and hire a private driver to drive me to school every day. It'll have lasers, a personal soda dispenser, a hot tub in the back, and probably even a butler!

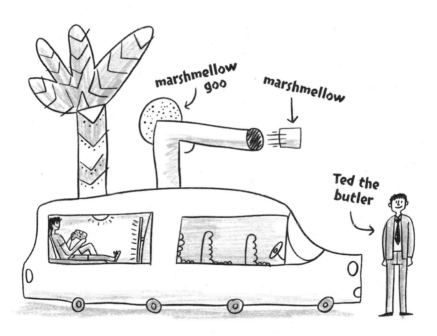

3

PIE FOR BREAKFAST

A few days later, at seven o'clock sharp on the first morning of summer break, Dad galloped through the second story of the Peach family's small-but-cozy house, blasting "Reveille" from his phone. Freddy rubbed his eyes. Fourth grade was officially over, and summer was already off to a rollicking start.

Dad's bugle wake-up music was most often used in the military, but it was also the ringtone for their father's morning alarm. Though Dad had never served in the armed forces, his father had—and Walter Peach had grown up surrounded by some of his father's old traditions. "Up and at 'em!" Dad cried while prancing up and down the hall. "All these peach pies are not gonna eat themselves!"

For Freddy, summer break *usually* meant ten weeks

filled with art projects, fort making, epic cardboard-sword-and-shield battles with his friends Ethan and Henry, brushing his teeth sometime after noon each day (if at all), reading his favorite illustrated random facts book every afternoon (as well as researching his *own* random facts), and cereal for lunch. This summer, of course, things would have been a bit different than usual: Freddy had a hunch summer school teachers didn't approve of kids who didn't brush their teeth.

But as he listened to his father whooping and hollering out in the hall, Freddy quickly came to the conclusion that this summer was going to be a whole lot *more* different than he ever could have anticipated. He quickly shoved his blanket to the side, and then tossed stuffed animals down into his little brother's bunk to try to wake him. But Herb could sleep through almost anything, which was fortunate, since he shared a room with Freddy.

Though Freddy and Lucy each had their own rooms when they were little, after Herb was born, the boys had been forced to share. Lucy—as the oldest—got the little bedroom to herself. Herb and Freddy squeezed into the big bedroom with bunk beds. Lately, Freddy and Herb's room was even more crowded than usual. Herb had been building up a whole bunch of "collections," and his piles and bins of stuff had expanded to the point that their room had almost no empty floor space left.

Freddy couldn't help wondering: since the million bucks was off-limits, if they made back some—or all—of this "fun money" operating the food truck, would they buy a bigger house, where he might get his very *own* room? If Freddy ever sold some of his art to a fancy gallery or some rich art-collector lady, he had plenty of ideas for how to spend his million bucks. A house with a basketball hoop, maybe. Definitely a pool. An elaborate, thirteen-story tree house. And a butler!

For now, though, he would settle for his personal grand prize: no summer school. Freddy had been trying to act like going to summer school was *no big deal.* But deep down, he hated that he was the only Peach kid being forced to go. He was the only member of the family who had ever failed a math test, which made him a full-on failure. He was all art and creativity and big ideas and fun facts, while his siblings and Dad were focused and sensible and *smart.* Dad was a big-shot geology professor. Lucy was a verified genius and sometimes did homework for *fun.* Herb went to a special math class at the university, to give him an extra challenge, because second grade was so easy for him. Everything came easily to the rest of his family. It seemed like *nothing* important came easily to Freddy. He was a plum in a whole family of Peaches.

Freddy climbed out of bed and sat on his brother. Herb *still* didn't stir. Freddy bounced on his brother's bed a few times, bonked him on the head with a stuffed ostrich, and finally gave up. Herb was always grumpy when he got up too early, anyway.

"Did Dad say *pie*?" Freddy wondered aloud, yawning as he stumbled into the hall. He sniffed the air, smelled something yummy, and made his way toward the kitchen. "For breakfast?"

Sure enough, the wooden kitchen counter was full-to-bursting with pies. Small pies, large pies, single-serve pie pockets, crustless pies, crumble-top pies, and several burnt-to-a-crisp pies. Freddy rubbed his eyes again, certain they must be deceiving him.

"Dig in!" Dad instructed with a slightly crazed look about him. Freddy had only seen his dad look like this after spending a long night in his university lab with heaps and piles of research figures.

"Dad?" Freddy asked. "Did you *bake* all these pies? *When?*"

"I stayed up all night. Just like at work, when I'm on a roll, I don't take breaks. We've no time to waste, Freddy-boy. The plan is for us to hit the road as soon as possible, so I wanted to start perfecting our recipe. We'll stop to do more pie research along the way, of course, but a pie's crust is its foundation. If the foundation is right, the pie will be all the better, and the mix of fat to flour is crucial for flakiness, and the ratio of . . ."

He droned on and on, making less and less sense with each word he said. Dad usually went to bed at 10:26 on the dot (immediately after the local news weather forecast) and got up at exactly 6:00. He was not the kind of guy who stayed up all night baking pies.

Lucy shuffled into the kitchen, stopping short when she saw their dad's collection of fresh-baked pies.

Freddy grabbed two forks and passed one to his sister. "It's research for the Great Peach Experiment," he explained, eagerly plunging his fork into the nearest pie. "Start eating. We've got a lot of tasting to do."

While Lucy and Freddy sampled pie, Dad talked through the summer plan, which did indeed sound very different from their *regular* summer plan. For the past few years, Dad had spent long summer days at the university, helping to oversee a bunch of graduate students' research projects. Lucy, Freddy, and Herb spent their summer breaks at the community center pool or roaming around the neighborhood, with Lucy in charge to help keep their lives somewhat organized.

For this summer adventure, Dad had written out a detailed route for their journey, along with a daily schedule of activities. It went as follows: They would spend the first weekend of summer break at home testing recipes, buying supplies, getting stuff packed for the trip, and painting and cleaning the food truck—which had sat in the driveway for the past few days, untouched. (The truck was apparently in "great working order and ready to roll," according to their dad, who knew nothing about food trucks.)

After that, they would visit a bunch of different cities that Dad had picked out, stopping for a few days in each to sell pie. According to Dad's schedule, every night would be dedicated to replenishing their supplies, rolling and baking crusts, and tidying up the food truck. Every morning they would finish making their pies for the day, drive to some special spot he had picked out in each city, and hang out in the food truck, selling slices of pie to strangers. There were no weekend days off in the schedule Dad had drawn up, and Freddy didn't see a whole lot of room for *fun*. But he hoped *that* part of this adventure was a given, and Dad had simply forgotten to write the fun stuff down.

The whole Great Peach Experiment would last four weeks. "A month should give us just enough time to test out this food truck experiment and see if we're any good at it. If we make some of our fun money back, well, then we'll figure out how to use the leftover funds."

Freddy and Lucy shared a look. The night before, the three Peach siblings had done a little research on food trucks together and discovered it was highly unlikely that they would make a fortune selling pies . . . but Freddy wasn't about to burst his dad's bubble. And even if making heaps of money during this experiment wasn't *likely*, it also wasn't *impossible*. So Freddy had every intention of helping his family do everything they needed to do to succeed—for Mom, obviously. But also to prove to Dad that spending time pursuing this wacky idea was worth it; that *they* were worth it.

Just then, Herb wandered into the kitchen, rubbing his eyes. His footie pajamas were too small—he'd had to cut off the feet to make them fit—but Herb refused to toss them. The youngest Peach never got rid of anything. He took one look at the counter full of pie, and then grabbed a spoon to help with the taste testing.

"If all goes well this summer, and we figure out how to make enough money on this crazy venture that we can call it a success," Dad added wistfully, "maybe it'll be time for me to consider whether there's a different kind of life out there for me—for us?"

Freddy's eyes went wide. Had Dad—in his own odd way—just suggested that if their food truck made enough money, he might consider leaving his job? That he might, finally, be able to spend more *fun* time with them? That he might take some time away from his research to have family dinners, go hiking, and maybe even sometimes be there to see them off in the morning before school? If that was what Dad was suggesting, Freddy was even *more* resolved to make this venture successful. "What would you consider 'enough money'?" Freddy asked, curious to see if his Dad's expectations lined up with reality.

"Well . . ." Dad scratched his head. "I suppose if we came home with ten thousand dollars or so in profits, I would consider that a success? It's less than my salary at the university, but it's not peanuts. It would be a good start, that's for sure."

Freddy nodded. *Ten thousand dollars.* That seemed doable, didn't it? How hard could it be to make ten thousand bucks selling pies?

Through a mouthful of peach filling, Herb asked, "How long do we have to make that much money?"

"A month," Dad told him.

Herb nodded, and judging by his far-off expression, Freddy could tell his little brother was doing mental math. "So, if we bring in $2,500 in profits each week," Herb said, "or about $350 per day, that would do it."

Freddy gaped at his little brother. How did Herb do that kind of math in his head so fast? But Herb was a math whiz, so Freddy knew those calculations must be correct. "We can do it," Freddy promised. He would make sure of it.

Dad went on, "The past few years have been hard on all of us, and I know work has been taking up a lot of my time. Perhaps . . ." He trailed off, shaking his head. "Well, let's just see how this goes first."

Ever since Mom died, Dad hadn't been around much. Freddy missed their family time. They used to have all kinds of fun traditions—building and flying homemade kites in the park on Sundays, first-Saturday-of-the-month slime-mixing stations, cupcake decorating competitions. All those things had disappeared along with Mom. Lucy had done her best to keep things as normal as possible, but there was only so much she could do. Except now, maybe, Dad was ready to help search for some of the missing parts of their family.

Freddy smiled at each of his siblings as he took another bite of pie. They could *do* this!

Dad blundered on. "We do have one more impor-tant thing to discuss as a family. I've been doing a bit of thinking, and I thought it might be fun if we each set some sort of goal for this summer."

Freddy lifted his eyebrows. Setting goals sounded suspiciously like *homework*.

"A plan, of sorts, to guide our experiment," Dad declared. "Of course, there should also be some room for surprises along the way. Like that time I *thought* I was getting a sediment core from the *Norwegian* Sea, but it turned out the core we opened was from the *North* Sea." He chuckled and drifted off, a slight smile tugging at the corners of his mouth. "Ah, yes, that was exciting. What I'm trying to say is, in addition to setting *goals* for the trip, there will also be plenty of room for serendipity this summer."

"Sara and who?" Herb asked. "Who's Ippity?"

"What's that now?" Dad asked.

"You said *Sara* and *Ippity*," Herb repeated. Dad stared at him, clearly not understanding. Herb asked, "Who are they?"

"Serendipity," Lucy explained. "It's a word that means a happy little accident—a fun surprise."

Through a mouthful of pie, Dad said, "I recently found out about a food truck festival in Delaware, Ohio, that I thought could be a good end point for our journey. The winning truck takes home a ten-thousand-dollar cash prize. If we won, that would certainly help to prove this experiment was *truly* worth it. The route I have planned will take us through Ohio anyway, so I was thinking we could make the festival a sort of *goal*. We can take a few weeks to get our business up and running, make some good money along the way, and then at the festival, we'll be able to test what we've learned during our experiment."

Freddy loved the idea of winning a food truck festival. This was exactly the kind of specific goal he could get on board with. Best of all, if they won, they'd be coming home with at *least* ten thousand dollars. Then dad would have no choice but to see this summer as a success! "I'm in," he said. "So how do they figure out who the food truck festival winner is?"

"An excellent question, Fred!" Dad said. "Each food truck that enters gets a score based on how much money they make during the festival, as well as being judged on customer service and taste."

"Got it," Freddy said, nodding seriously. That seemed simple enough. They could practice all of those things—making money, baking tasty pies, and being nice to customers—over the next few weeks. "What will we do with the money when we win?"

Dad took a deep breath. "Well, I suppose we'd have

to figure that out. Perhaps we could use it to do a couple of the other things your Mom always talked about doing together: unique trips, big adventures, maybe take a cheese class."

"A cheese class?" Freddy asked, lifting his eyebrows.

"You learn about and taste different types of cheese," Dad explained. "That's just one idea, of course. We can figure out how to spend the winnings together."

"Let's worry about winning first, okay?" Lucy suggested.

"Yes," Dad said, nodding solemnly. "Yes, that's a good point. Now, what's everyone else's personal goal for the trip? Winning the Ohio Food Truck Festival can be a goal we all work toward as a family. But I'd like each of you to come up with a goal of your own, to make this experience more meaningful."

"I know!" Herb said, jumping up and down. "I know my goal. I love swimming. And since we aren't going to get a pool for the backyard yet, can we try to swim every day during our trip? Will our hotels have indoor pools or outdoor pools, do you think?"

Dad stared at him blankly for a moment. Then he whistled, and said, "It seems I forgot to tell you the best part of this trip!" Freddy had a feeling Dad's *best part* was going to be anything but. He turned to witness Lucy's reaction to whatever Dad was about to say. "We're going to be camping this summer! It's much cheaper than staying in hotels, so our fun money will last longer. Plus, this way, we can be footloose and fancy-free, and we'll sleep under the stars each night. Doesn't that sound like fun?"

"We're *camping*?" Lucy asked. Freddy coughed to hide a laugh. The look on his sister's face was *priceless*! "For real?"

Dad grinned. "Indeed. Some of my fondest memories from childhood are from the summer camping trips my cousins and I took. Every night, we found a new place to call home. We'll set up shop in campgrounds where we can sleep beside lakes or rivers, and I'm pretty sure there are even a few campgrounds with outdoor pools. So, Herb," he said, barreling on, "your summer goal to swim every day is perfectly valid. My hypothesis is, that should be doable."

Freddy quickly spoke up. It was clear that Lucy needed a few minutes to collect herself after Dad's latest surprise. "I've got a goal. So, there's this app Ethan told me about that helps you find really cool, hidden roadside attractions—stuff like the world's largest ball of twine. Did you know there's not one, but *two* huge cherry pie pans we could stop and see in Michigan? And get this:

there are, like, *ten* giant Paul Bunyan statues around the country. Maybe we could get that app on your phone and make it a goal to stop and see some of the weird stuff we pass along the way?"

"What a wonderful way for us to enjoy the journey!" Dad crooned.

Freddy snorted out a laugh. Their dad was acting like a total goof; for the first time in two years, he was full of smiles and enthusiasm. Freddy loved it.

Dad added, "That's a fun goal, Freddy. Your mother would definitely like that idea."

Freddy felt his face flush. He had to choke down the bite of pie he'd just popped into his mouth. "What about you, Lucy?" he asked, hoping to shift the attention to his sister.

Dad nodded. "Yes. Lucy: Do you have a goal for our trip? What do you want to do this summer, more than anything?"

"No goal," she muttered. "Honestly, the only thing I *wanted* was to have a normal summer. My *goal* would be to go to the pool with my friends, and hang out in hammocks by the rose garden, and go on bike rides with lots of ice cream stops. And I want time to sit around and read, without any other stuff getting in my way." She sighed and dropped her fork on the counter, where it landed with a plunk. "But it looks like I'm going to be standing around in a hot truck, making pies instead."

"Interesting," Dad said, seemingly oblivious to Lucy's frustration. "Now, regarding this *reading* goal: can you be a little more specific? I'm sure you understand the importance of setting *clear* goals with definable outcomes, Lucy. Vague goals don't get you anywhere."

"Fine," Lucy huffed. "My goal is to read every book on the seventh-grade summer reading list, even though my language arts teacher told us we only have to read two. Is *that* clear enough for you?"

"Perfectly," Dad said with a distant smile. "Now . . . who's ready for more pie?"

Suggested Reading List
for Incoming Seventh Graders

Research has shown that thirty minutes of daily reading in the summer helps build reading skills and comprehension! Please ~~select at least two novels of your choice to~~ read over the summer.

all of these books ^

- *The War That Saved My Life* by Kimberly Brubaker Bradley
- *Brown Girl Dreaming* by Jacqueline Woodson
- The Shadow Children series by Margaret Peterson Haddix
- *Refugee* by Alan Gratz
- *The Outsiders* by S. E. Hinton
- *The Penderwicks* by Jeanne Birdsall
- *One Crazy Summer* by Rita Williams-Garcia
- *Fish in a Tree* by Lynda Mullaly Hunt
- *The Remarkable Journey of Coyote Sunrise* by Dan Gemeinhart
- *Orphan Island* by Laurel Snyder
- *Amal Unbound* by Aisha Saeed
- *A Tree Grows in Brooklyn* by Betty Smith
- *Rebound* by Kwame Alexander

- *March* by John Lewis
- *The Seventh Wish* by Kate Messner
- *The Bridge Home* by Padma Venkatraman
- *The Thing About Jellyfish* by Ali Benjamin
- *Jellicoe Road* by Melina Marchetta
- *Island of the Blue Dolphins* by Scott O'Dell
- *Echo* by Pam Muñoz Ryan
- *Ghost* by Jason Reynolds
- *Genesis Begins Again* by Alicia D. Williams
- *Insignificant Events in the Life of a Cactus* by Dusti Bowling
- *A Night Divided* by Jennifer A. Nielsen
- *Amina's Voice* by Hena Khan
- *The Ethan I Was Before* by Ali Standish
- *Breadcrumbs* by Anne Ursu
- *Julie of the Wolves* by Jean Craighead George
- *The Parker Inheritance* by Varian Johnson
- *Front Desk* by Kelly Yang

4

HIDDEN TREASURE

Herb's tummy hurt. Though the youngest Peach had always liked pie, now that he'd been eating it for almost two hours straight, he didn't think he ever wanted to eat it again. Unfortunately, Dad had announced that the Peaches would be eating nothing *but* pie for the next month, and no one could tell if he was joking or not. Dad wasn't a joking kind of guy.

Herb had always believed a day filled with dessert alone would be delicious, but after just one morning shoving his face full of gooey, sticky peach pie, he was actually craving something not-so-sweet. At times like this, when he'd had too much sugar and his belly felt squirmy, he thought about one of his mom's favorite sayings: "When life gives you lemons, make iced tea."

Herb loved that his mom had always looked at things

a little differently than the rest of the world. She said that lemonade—the star of the original saying, *When life gives you lemons, make lemonade*—was too sweet for her taste. (Herb agreed, but if he was being honest, he didn't much like iced tea, either.) A few years ago, Herb and his siblings had gotten Mom's favorite saying embroidered on a pillow for her as a Christmas gift, to try to help cheer her up during all those long weeks of chemotherapy. Now the pillow sat unused on Mom's favorite reading chair, as a reminder of all the sour lemons life had thrown at the Peach family these past few years.

That morning, as Herb rubbed his sore belly, Lucy quietly slipped him a bowl of carrot sticks. The veggies helped settle his tummy enough that he could squeeze in just a little more peach pie.

After tasting every single one of the sample pies Dad had baked, the kids had all decided that the medium-thick crust was the best-quality crust for selling by the slice—it wasn't soggy and didn't fall apart when you cut into it. There was some discussion about whether traditional crust or buttery crumble made a better topping. This discussion led to a bit of a disagreement, which turned into a full-blown fight. Finally, Freddy suggested they could make some pies with *crumb* topping and others with *crust* topping and test to see which one was more popular with customers. That compromise calmed everyone down for a bit.

Freddy had spent part of the morning doing some more research online at the family computer in the dining room, and he had found several hole-in-the-wall pie shops that he thought they should stop and visit along their route. Though these stops weren't included on Dad's original schedule, Freddy had pointed out that it would be important to stop and do some pie-tasting research along the way. Somehow, Herb's big brother had smooth-talked Dad into seeing things his way, so now their first stop on the journey would be at Betty's Pies, just north of their hometown of Duluth, Minnesota. Freddy had also found several other pie shops he was eager to stop at throughout Minnesota, Wisconsin, Illinois, and Michigan, but Dad hadn't agreed to those detours quite yet.

"Get this: there's one place that bakes their pies in a *paper bag*," Freddy called into the kitchen from where he sat in front of the computer. "That's pretty cool. Another place is known for butterscotch pie, which sounds interesting and also is probably pretty easy to make. And here's something good to know: Michigan doesn't just have the world's largest cherry pie *pan*, they're also really into cherry pie. That's because of Michigan cherries. We probably want to have cherry pie on our menu if we stop in Michigan. I didn't bother looking for any pie places to stop at beyond Michigan," he was saying as he rejoined the family in the kitchen. "I figure we better have our menu pretty well sorted out by then, or we won't have any hope of winning that food truck festival in Ohio."

Dad suddenly yawned and swayed, catching the edge of the counter to keep himself from falling over. "I'll tell you what. I'm pooped," he said. "Let's head outside and get started painting and cleaning the truck, before I collapse."

Though most food trucks used special wraps for their name and logo, Dad had explained, the Peaches didn't have time to wait for a custom food truck wrap to be completed. Instead, they would be customizing the bright peachy-orange-colored truck with painted-on, swirly black-and-green stencil letters and a giant dancing peach sticker. Hoping to help, Herb had suggested they paint dragons or flames or *something* exciting on the side of the truck, but he was outvoted.

While Dad and Lucy bickered over how to work the paint sprayer, Herb and Freddy set to work cleaning out the inside of the truck. They each got a big bucket of sudsy water and a few sponges. To make the job more appealing, Dad told them they were allowed to have soap fights while they cleaned. It was okay if soap and water sploshed on the floor, he said; the most important thing was that they scrub the space from top to bottom. *How* they got it clean was up to them, and this kind of freedom was exciting to Herb.

Dad had also promised that if they found any treasures while they were cleaning, they could keep them. So far, Herb had found almost three dollars in loose change, an old bandanna, a funny grocery list, and a still-in-the-wrapper chocolate bar! This was his lucky day.

The two boys scrubbed and explored and scrubbed some more, cranking up the music inside the truck while they worked. They soaped up the countertops, emptied the fridge, and scraped charred bits off the top of the stove. Then Herb attached sudsy sponges to his knees to scrub the floor. He swished and slid back and forth, leaving soapy trails across the floor of the truck.

Herb was back in the far corner of the truck, near the pantry area, when he noticed a piece of cloth sticking out from under one of the low shelves. He grabbed the fabric and tugged. It felt like an old T-shirt, soft and worn. But no matter how hard he pulled, the piece of cloth wouldn't come loose. "Freddy!" he cried, trying to get his brother's attention over the loud music. Freddy was dancing, tapping his soap-filled sponges on the counters along with the beat. "Freddy!" Herb called again. "Help me move this shelf."

Freddy slid over, and then leaned his whole weight against the shelf. It was screwed in place, just like everything in the food truck (so that it wouldn't go flying around when they were on the road), but Freddy was able to shift it just enough for Herb to reach his tiny fingers in and wiggle the fabric free. He pulled it out and was disappointed to see it wasn't anything exciting—just an old, dirty, torn-up T-shirt. He scooped it up, preparing to toss it in the big trash bag. But then, just as Freddy was dancing away, Herb felt the fabric move. Startled, he let the ball of soft cotton fall open. When it did, several tiny noses poked out of the folds. It seemed that three teeny-weeny mice babies had made their home in an old T-shirt inside the food truck!

Fascinated, Herb settled down on the nubby silver floor, cradling the little pouch full of critters in the palms of his hands. "Hello," he whispered. One of the mice twitched its nose. Carefully, Herb tucked the edges of the fabric up and around the three little mice, capturing them inside the soft pouch. With a smile, he cupped his newfound treasure in his hands and headed toward the back door of the truck. "Dad?" he called out. "You promised I can keep *anything* I find, right?"

"Whatever you find in there while you're cleaning," his dad said distractedly, "is yours."

Herb grinned. Three mice of his very own, to keep! Because a promise was a promise. "I'm going to keep you safe and happy, little mice," he whispered to the little critters. "I promise."

THE MIDWEST

From the Sketchbook of Freddy Peach:
HOW TO SPEND A MILLION DOLLARS

When I sell a bunch of my art to some crazy rich lady, I'm going to build a moat around our house and hire a footman whose only job is to raise and lower the front drawbridge. He would also have a giant sword and armor, because that would look fierce.

5

THE FINAL DETAILS

"I have a question," Lucy said to her dad later that night, after she'd gotten her brothers settled into bed. As always, she'd read Herb a chapter of *The Penderwicks* (the book they were reading aloud together), and then tucked his favorite stuffed pig under his pillow, just the way he liked. "So this food truck experiment of yours is supposed to last a month, right?"

"*Ours,*" Dad corrected.

"Huh?"

"It's *our* experiment, Lulu," Dad pointed out. "Not just mine. We're doing this in Mom's honor, as a family."

"Okay . . . *ours.*" Lucy sighed, still not entirely convinced this was a sane or full-fledged idea that would actually stick. "You still haven't explained how you're suddenly able to take all this time off work. You *never* take vacation. Science conferences don't count."

Lucy thought about the only trips they'd taken after Mom died. For Dad's work, they'd visited a couple of fun *places*, like San Francisco, San Diego, and San Antonio. But none of those trips had actually *been* any fun at all. When they got to San Francisco, they didn't get to visit the redwood forest or traipse across the Golden Gate Bridge, as they'd all been hoping and expecting. Instead, the three Peach kids sat at a round table in a windowless banquet hall in a Ramada Inn, snacking on a platter of cookies while they colored pictures of famous monuments.

In San Diego they didn't go to the world famous San Diego Zoo (like Dad had promised) or even so much as dip their feet in the ocean. Instead, they watched a documentary about zoo animals in a stale hotel room while their father oohed and aahed over chunks of soil someone had pulled out of the ocean floor. (Freddy had done some digging, and helpfully explained to his siblings, "Those long tubes of soil are called cores, and they help scientists understand climate change and other stuff.")

When they drove into San Antonio, the Peach kids had pressed their noses against the glass windows, peering at the Alamo as they drove past on their way to the convention center that would host the Mysteries of Paleoclimate! conference. But they hadn't stopped to get out and explore, so that trip had been another bust.

"Ah, yes," Dad said, pulling his eyebrows together. "Yes, it has been a while, hasn't it?"

Lucy snapped, "You haven't taken a single day off work in two years. Not since Mom died." In the first few weeks after they lost Mom forever, it had seemed like Dad might be capable of handling everything. That he'd be willing and able to pick up the bruised and smushed remnants of their family and try to reshape them into something new. Because Mom had died from cancer, he'd said at the time, there was plenty of time for him to prepare. He'd been warned it was coming, and that was supposed to have made her death easier to handle.

Lucy had *also* had time to prepare; yet she never felt that made Mom's passing any easier. In some ways, *knowing* what was coming had been worse—because she'd had all those months to worry about what was going to happen, and when. And then, after it *actually* happened and Mom was gone for good, Lucy was faced with the reality of the situation and the day-to-day absence that no one could have prepared her for.

Nobody had been able to warn her about all the days she'd *forget*, come home from school, and—for one pass-ing second—think about sitting down to tell her mom all about her day. Then she'd remember, and that rock would drop in her stomach again, and she'd start the cycle all over.

But the hardest part was watching how Dad dealt with his grief in the first weeks after Mom's death. It made Lucy feel like she wasn't *allowed* to be sad. His way of coping made Lucy feel like *knowing* Mom was going to die should have made it all easier somehow.

Those first few weeks after the funeral had been awful. But then, about three weeks after she died, Dad disappeared, too. That's when life got even worse. Dad's sadness caught up with him, and he buried himself in work to hide from the reality of their situation and—*poof!*—evaporated from daily life altogether.

That's when Lucy took over. Watching how her Dad unraveled in the months that followed, she had wished *she* was allowed to wallow and be sad, too. But Lucy had two little brothers that needed someone to take care of them, and no one else had volunteered to do the job. Their only real family—Great Aunt Lucinda, who was Dad's aunt and the person Lucy had been named after—lived in a giant mansion across town, and she had the Peach kids over sometimes to play cards or eat brunch with her and her collection of small, naughty dogs. Aunt Lucinda was kind and fun and one of Lucy's favorite people on earth, but she was also *old*, so it's not as if she could do much to help. So Lucy had toughened up and dealt with the day-to-day stuff as best she could.

"Has it been that long? Not since your mother died? Really?" Dad blanched as this fact hit him square on. "Well, as you know, work has been crazy. But the thing is, I've been due for a sabbatical for quite some time now."

"What's a sabbatical?" Lucy asked, grabbing a container of strawberries out of the fridge. She washed them, then began to slice them into a bowl for the morning. Herb and Freddy loved having fresh-cut strawberries to put on their cereal. It was a sneaky way to get them to eat more fruit.

"Every few years, I'm granted a leave of absence from the university," Dad explained, "to work on my research and writing and take a break from the everyday things that come up with teaching and my graduate students and so forth."

Lucy looked up from the cutting board and cocked her head. "So let me get this straight: In theory, you could have taken a leave of absence from work *anytime* over the past two years? To have more time at home, and maybe take one of the fun family trips you promised, or even just be around for dinner a few nights a week?"

"I suppose, well . . . yes, I suppose that's true," Dad

said, not seeming to notice Lucy's tone of voice. "But I guess the good news is, I have that time now."

Lucy nodded. That was something at least. It had taken nearly two years, but their dad finally realized how much he was missing. "I'm glad you finally decided to take the time."

"To be totally honest, Lucy"—Dad cleared his throat—"I'm going to tell you something that I'd prefer you not share with your brothers. I—well, I wouldn't want them to worry."

Lucy stood totally still, strawberry in hand, waiting for whatever it was her father had to say. She hated secrets, but she'd found it was usually better to be *in* on one than to be the one left *out*. Though she wasn't sure that was going to be true in this case.

"You see," Dad said, refusing to make eye contact with her, "the head of my department felt now might be a good time for me to take a short break. She and I agreed that there's never a *good* time to be away, but this is as good a time as any. She thought it would be best for everyone if I take this summer off to figure some things out."

"So," Lucy began carefully, as she tried to understand what her dad was telling her, "this is a *forced* sabbatical? Your boss *made* you take this summer off?" She paused and stared at him. "Are you still getting paid?"

"I am getting paid." Dad nodded slowly. "And yes, I was asked to take some time off, but . . ." He shook his head, looking like he was at a loss for words.

Lucy set the knife on the counter and considered this new piece of information. The so-called Great Peach Experiment that Freddy and Herb were so excited about? It had only come up because their dad had basically been told he wasn't *allowed* to go to work for the summer.

Dad hadn't *chosen* this. A summer spent together, working toward a fun family goal, had been *forced* on him.

"So you didn't have any choice in the matter?" Lucy asked. "You're only spending the summer with us because you literally don't have *anything* else to do?"

Dad winced. "Now, Lucy, that's not entirely fair. Don't think of it like that. Let's think of this trip as a kind of serendipity. I got the summer off, and I'm trying to make the most of it." He sighed, dropped his elbows on the table, and rested his forehead in his palms. "The thing is, I realize we haven't had much fun time together as a family these past few years. I see this summer as a chance to change that. And in the process, we can fulfill one of your mother's dreams."

Lucy heard what her dad was saying, but she was struggling to believe it. She was trying to be positive about this trip; really, she was. But it was very difficult to watch her brothers getting so excited about something, knowing full well that her dad was sure to abandon ship when the going got rough. As soon as he had the chance to disappear again, he would. She'd seen it happen, over and over again for the past two years. All the choir concerts he'd promised to be there for, the family walks on weekends, the weekly dinner as a family . . . none of it had worked out at all the way he'd promised it would. When it was Mom-and-Dad they had *always* been there, but now that it was just-Dad, there was always some excuse.

Still, she didn't have much choice but to go along with this very risky whim. And if she really *had* to be a part of this family experiment, the least she could do was try to make the most of it. Maybe what Freddy told her and Herb earlier that night was true. *Maybe,* Freddy had said, *if this experiment goes well, Dad will decide he wants to spend more time with us.* Lucy could only hope her brother's wish would come true.

She plucked a berry slice out of the bowl and chewed it thoughtfully. "Okay." She sighed. "Fair enough. But here's another question: Do you honestly think we can learn everything we need to know about running a food truck in the next few days? And be ready to compete in the Food Truck Festival in less than a month? I imagine it's not a simple thing."

Dad finally looked up and began to laugh. "Of course not! Your mom actually did a lot of research for us before she died," he said excitedly. "I've just had to put her plans and idea in motion." He then went on to tell Lucy that all those evenings she thought her dad had been busy working extra *extra* late the past few weeks, he had actually already *been* on his sabbatical. He hadn't been at the lab; he'd been researching and completing all the necessary steps to get their food truck up and running. "I've already secured all the permits and licenses we need, and sorted out the other legal stuff," he told her. He had also taken an online class on food truck management, shadowed a down-town food truck owner over the course of several busy afternoons, and ensured the truck he'd ordered was up to code.

"So glad you're on top of everything," Lucy grumbled, frustrated. Her dad had been lying to them for weeks! "Sounds like you've got all the most important stuff covered."

"Thank you!" Dad said, beaming. "I really think I do!"

A moment later, Herb called down the stairs, "Can I have a glass of water? My throat is itchy."

Lucy glanced at her dad, who was now hunched over his laptop and had—it seemed—suddenly gone deaf.

Herb yelled, "Helloooooo? Luuuucy?"

Lucy slid the bowl of strawberries into the fridge, then filled a plastic cup with water and one ghost-shaped ice cube. Just the way Herb liked it. Then she headed upstairs to tuck her brother in tight.

Dear Great Aunt Lucinda,

   I'm sorry we didn't have time to come over to say goodbye in person before we left. I wish you could have tasted a slice of your famous peach pie—Dad's actually a pretty good baker. Who knew?? As soon as we get back from this food truck road trip, I'll bring you a piece so you can taste it, and so we can get our Hearts tournament (vs. the boys!) going again. Say hi to the dogs. I miss them already.

Love,

Lucy

PS: I hope you find some other card-playing friends to fill in for me and my brothers while we're gone—but don't let them eat all that yummy chocolate your friend sent from Switzerland, ok??

6

BETTY'S PIES

First thing Monday morning, as soon as the truck was prepped and packed and their pie recipe perfected, the massive Peach Pie Truck rumbled out of the driveway, heading toward Betty's Pies on the North Shore of Lake Superior. Though their dad wasn't usually an off-the-planned-route kind of guy, Freddy had managed to convince him that it made sense to kick off their summer experiment by driving thirty minutes north so they could have a bellyful of Minnesota's own world-famous pie-for-breakfast.

When they arrived at Betty's, it took a ridiculously long time for their Dad to park the food truck in the restaurant's lot. Freddy could tell Dad hadn't gotten used to driving their new vehicle yet. First, he took the turn too tightly. Then he hit a patch of grass and bumped over a curb. Eventually he was in such a pickle that he had to back out of the parking lot and go at it again. This process went on for a good five minutes. By the time he finally managed to ease the giant peach beast around the corner, traffic had backed up on the highway and several cars were honking at him in a very un-Minnesota-nice way.

Inside the restaurant, Freddy couldn't wait to share the results of some of the pie research he'd done that weekend. He told his family that Betty's was famous for cream pies and crunch pies. "I say we try the turtle, coconut, maple walnut, French cherry, caramel apple crunch, and five-layer chocolate pie. A slice of each of those, and maybe we can also order some of the plain fruit pies, all to share?"

Lucy had her nose buried in one of the many books she planned to read during the trip, and barely looked up long enough to grunt out something that sounded like an approval. Herb and Dad both shrugged. Freddy had to pinch his own leg to keep himself from growling in frustration. It seemed to him that no one else in the family truly *cared* about this experiment's success. Were the other Peaches planning to go into this summer adventure without any kind of game plan? What kind of entrepreneur, he wanted to scream out, just jumps into a business venture without doing some research, testing, and hypothesizing about what products would be most likely to sell?

Freddy had visited their mom's lab plenty of times when he was little, and he knew that the scientists she worked with did all *kinds* of tests and experiments before they could move to the next step of a product's development—that was the fun part, Mom had always said. Their food truck venture wasn't *that* different from one of their mom's experiments. He knew there must be a process they should follow, and he wasn't even considered the smart one in the family.

When their pie order arrived, everyone took a slice and dug in. Then they passed the pieces left to right so they could sample each of Betty's most famous creations. Freddy took notes as he ate, and began to brainstorm some fun flavor combinations they could try offering on the Peach Pie Truck menu once business was really rolling.

By the time they got to their fourth plate pass, Herb shoved his plate away and groaned. "No more pie."

"Nonsense," Dad said, pushing Herb's plate back in front of him. "This pie is fantastic. Keep eating."

Herb moaned. Lucy glanced up. She folded the corner of her page and set her book to the side just as Herb proclaimed, "My tummy hurts."

"Don't be silly. It's important not to give up when the going gets rough," Dad said cheerfully. Freddy caught Lucy glaring at their dad from across the table, but Dad was totally oblivious. He nudged Herb's fork and nodded. "Come on, Herbie. We all need to do our part."

"Mmmnnn," Herb muttered. He poked his fork into the slice of five-layer chocolate pie and scowled. "Pie is poopy."

"Dad," Lucy said calmly, nibbling a chunk of crust, "don't forget about Herb's sensitive stomach. He always gets sick when he has too much sugar."

"Only one way a sensitive stomach will get stronger: challenge it," Dad said, plopping a chunk of Old-Fashioned Apple into his mouth. "Put your belly to the test, Herb. Ignore the pain. Shove in a little more pie and *force* your tummy to tolerate it!"

"But—" Lucy began.

Before she could finish her sentence, Herb jumped up from the table. He raced across the restaurant, holding a fist in front of his face as he beelined for the bathroom.

"I think Herb's gonna lose it," Freddy said. Then he grabbed Herb's half-full plate and drove his fork into the five-layer chocolate pie. With a shrug, he scooped up a huge bite. "More for me."

From the Sketchbook of Freddy Peach:
PIES TO TRY

Strawberry Rhubarb

Peach

Key Lime

Boston Cream

(is this considered PIE or CAKE?)

Pumpkin

Turtle

French Silk (my fave!)

Raisin (not my fave)

THE APPLE PIE FAMILY:

Cheddar Apple

Dutch Apple

Apple Crumble

Apple Crisp

Plain Old Apple

Apple Brown Betty

Caramel Apple

7

TRUCK TROUBLE

Though riding in the bright peach truck was hot (no air-conditioning) and deeply embarrassing (especially after their dad put on his giant, brimmed sun hat), Lucy found herself actually enjoying the drive from Betty's Pies to Minneapolis. She was the only Peach kid tall enough to sit up front next to Dad, while her brothers had to wedge their bodies into the strange and uncomfortable-looking passenger seats behind them. Herb's new pet mice were nestled into the only leftover space between the two back seats, looking confused and miserable inside their little glass fish tank enclosure.

Lucy had already decided she liked road trips. It wasn't often that she got four and a half hours to sit and read without having to deal with one of her brothers' messes or listening to them bicker about which shape of noodles she should cook for lunch. And this was the first summer since their mom got sick that Dad was making any kind of effort to spend quality time together as a family. Even though the time off had been *forced* on him, Dad had chosen to spend the time with *them*... and that was something.

For the past two summers, Lucy had been tasked with taking care of her brothers while their dad disappeared. But this summer, whether he'd realized it yet or not, Dad had become part of the equation again. And Lucy planned to make the most of her newfound free time while pursuing her summer reading goal.

Two hours into their journey, she was completely immersed in her third novel of summer break—*A Night Divided*—when the truck lurched and began to make a disturbing *thump thump thump thump* sound. Based on the way the truck was bouncing along at an odd slant, Lucy had a pretty good feeling one of the tires on the "good as new" truck had gone flat.

"Whoa, Nelly," Dad said, slowing the truck. He held the wheel steady, guiding their giant vehicle toward the side of the road. Lucy glanced out the window and saw that they were in the middle of nowhere. There was a billboard advertising a corn maze—COME BY FOR SOME GOOD, CORNY FUN IN THE MIDDLE OF NOWHERE!—but

other than that, there was nothing but fields for as far as the eye could see. Dad eased the truck onto the shoulder and came to a stop. Then he climbed out of the truck to investigate. "Back in a jiffy!" he called out to the kids with a quick tip of his hat.

Freddy and Herb both scrambled into the front seat, then hopped over Lucy to get to the truck's passenger-side door. Both boys spilled out onto the shoulder, jumping and playing happily in the tall grass along the side of the highway. "Can I let my mice out to run for a little bit?" Herb called out to Lucy.

"Do you have a leash?" she asked in reply. She had no intention of actually letting her brother release the mice in the grass on the side of the road. That experiment certainly wouldn't end well, and Herb would have a full-on meltdown if he lost them—or anything else he considered a prized possession. His collections were very important to him; ever since Mom had died, he'd refused to throw anything away. Lucy knew letting go was hard, so she tried to be patient with her little brother. "Or maybe one of those plastic hamster balls, to keep them contained?"

Herb looked confused for a second, but then he shrugged. "I forgot," he said sadly. "Oh well, they can just stay in the truck with you."

While her brothers stomped and danced in the long grass on the side of the highway, Lucy took a deep breath, considering her next move. On the one hand, she *could* be a good team player and get out of the truck to help her dad. She and her best friend, Maren, had taught themselves how to change a tire the previous summer. It was one of those things they believed a person should know how to do, so they'd taken it upon themselves to learn.

On the other hand, she was curious to see how her dad would handle the situation. Walter Peach was incredibly smart and had achieved great success in his career. But when it came to the puzzle of life's basic challenges, he sometimes seemed to be missing a few key pieces. Lucy already took care of her siblings most of the time; she couldn't babysit her dad, too.

Lucy rolled the window down the rest of the way and settled into her seat, resting her feet on the dash. She decided to see how things would play out *without* her getting involved, for once. Through the open window, she could hear her brothers chatting away while they lunged and karate-kicked each other in the grassy space along the side of the road. Herb's tummy troubles seemed to have improved after Lucy had ordered him a turkey sandwich at Betty's Pies.

While they battled, Freddy spouted off a collection of random facts about mice: "Did you know there are thirty-eight known species of mice? They're usually nocturnal, so they prefer to play at night. Also, their teeth never stop growing. *Never*, Herb. So if your mice don't get enough stuff to chew on, they could grow vampire teeth that stick out of their mouths and then they'll eat us all in our sleep." Lucy found it fascinating that Freddy was an endless fountain of useless facts about nearly everything. She listened as he rambled on. "Did you know mice can squeeze through a gap that's only as wide as a pencil? In some parts of the world, mice are considered a special treat, and people eat them for protein."

When she'd finally had enough of her brother's mouse facts, Lucy called out, "What seems to be the trouble, Dad?"

"Well," Dad replied, "I think I'm going to need to do a bit of preliminary research and see if we can identify the problem."

Lucy rolled her eyes. Her dad approached nearly every problem using the scientific method:

1. Ask a question.
2. Do background research.
3. Construct a hypothesis.
4. Test with an experiment.
5. Is the procedure working? If not, repeat steps 1–4. If yes, carry on.
6. Analyze data and draw conclusions.
7. Do the results align with the hypothesis?
8. Analyze and communicate results.

This process was great for lab work. But she'd found that this approach didn't always allow her father to bend and flex enough when faced with real-world challenges. Through the side window, Lucy could see her dad scanning every inch of the truck. "I don't think it's a belt," he muttered. Lucy rolled her eyes. She was pretty certain her dad knew absolutely nothing about the inner workings of food trucks, or even cars—real *or* toy.

"It doesn't look like we hit an animal," he mused.

"My guess is, our problem is a tire," Dad said, stating his hypothesis.

"Bingo," Lucy whispered. She paged through the truck's manual, which she found in the glove box, and discovered that the spare tire ought to be tucked inside a special compartment in the floor at the back of the truck.

Dad paced back and forth, using a little silver pressure gauge to test each of the tires. Judging from the way the truck had bumped and thumped before they pulled over, Lucy knew one of the tires probably *looked* pretty flat and he likely didn't even need to check the pressure to see where the problem was—but her dad wasn't the type to make assumptions without gathering evidence. He *would*, it seemed, buy a food truck on a lark, but that was a whole other ball of wax.

"A*ha!*" Dad cried out finally. "I believe the problem is our front right tire."

Lucy giggled. "A solid hypothesis," she muttered.

Dad stood stock-still, staring at the front of the truck for a very long time. "How are we going to fix this?" he asked quietly.

"Maybe we should call someone?" Freddy suggested.

"That's expensive and cuts into our summer earnings," Dad said, stroking his chin. "Perhaps we could try patching it?" He hemmed and hawed, then said, "Worth a try."

He began riffling through the truck, apparently trying to find something he could use to try to patch the tire. He came up empty-handed. Another ten minutes passed, during which he stared at the truck without testing any solutions at all. "Maybe I should just try driving on it, to see if it's still causing problems?" he finally said.

"Can I pee out here in the grass?" Herb hollered, but got no answer.

Lucy realized they would very likely be stuck on the side of the road for the next six days if someone didn't step in and *do* something. She realized she had a choice to make: she could help her mixed-up mess of a family, or let everything fall apart again.

Lucy set her book to the side and hopped out of the truck.

"Lucy! Do you have a hypothesis?" Dad asked. "I think it's the tire. But I haven't been able to gather quite enough data to draw a full conclusion and solve the problem."

"Sometimes," Lucy answered through gritted teeth, "a flat tire is just a flat tire." Then she popped open the truck's big back door, dragged the enormous spare out of its hiding spot, and got to work.

HOW TO SPEND A MILLION DOLLARS

When I'm a millionaire, I'm going to have a private pool for Herb (and me) that is bigger and better than the snooty country club pool. With waterslides! Fountains! A swim-up ice cream bar! Live music! Underwater TVs!

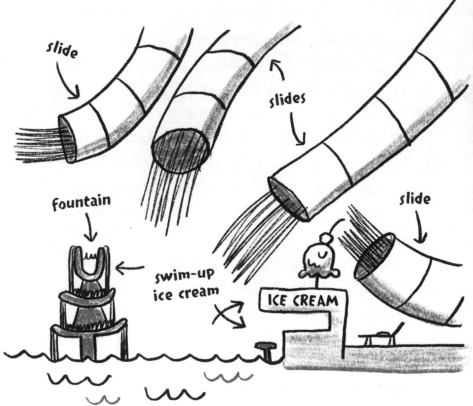

How Dad spent Mom's million? On a busted food truck.

Dear Great Aunt Lucinda,

This food truck experiment—it's crazy, right? Do I need to worry that Dad has gone totally nuts? I know you can't actually answer any of my questions (since we don't have an address you can write back to, and Dad won't let us use his phone—it's for "work and roadside emergencies only"), but I'll keep writing you old-fashioned postcards from our trip, so you can maybe send help if it seems like we really need it. Has Dasher stolen and buried any of your wigs again lately? Haha!

Much love,
Lucy

8

HERB'S COLLECTION

They had been away from home less than a day, but Herb already missed his stuff. For the past few years—almost as far back as he could remember, really—Herb had been cultivating a special collection of treasures that he watched over and cherished. It was his garden of goodies. His mound of magic. His pile of precious.

Freddy too often told Herb his stuff was just junk.

Lucy had told him he'd created a fire hazard.

But Herb loved and carefully guarded every last item in his collection. There were nearly two dozen once-lost-but-now-found stuffed animals that he'd rescued from various places around town. Several had been forgotten by their kids at the playground. The purple bunny he'd found in a puddle in the grocery store parking lot. A fuzzy green frog had been left for dead on the sidewalk near the bus stop. The headless giraffe had appeared—like magic—on their front lawn when last winter's snow melted. Each time Herb saw a stuffy in need, he picked it up and bathed it, nursed it back to good health, and added it to his box of friends in the back corner of his room. He knew it was his job to protect them.

Then there were the art projects: boxes and boxes of beautiful art projects that Herb had found—thrown carelessly away by kids at school. Whenever he found a lovely picture or diorama or clay creation tossed in the trash, Herb rescued it from the bin and brought it home to be treasured as part of the collection.

Herb had also started moving all the old clothes that no longer fit into his stash. He didn't like to see things he cared about disappear for good. He'd never tell Lucy, but Herb had also taken a bunch of singleton mittens from the lost and found at school on the afternoon their school secretary was planning to throw them away.

There were also boxes and containers filled to bursting with:

- Cool pine cones and rusted matchbox cars he'd collected at the park
- Empty Thinking Putty tins
- Marbles

- Holey socks
- His mom's nearly empty shampoo and hair cream bottles (He liked to smell those to help remember her.)
- Expired Box Tops

Herb was the keeper of all kinds of lost and forgotten treasures.

Though he missed his stuff at home, he was thrilled that he'd have a chance to start up a *new* collection on the road. His first major win was finding the mouse family. This was the most exciting—and challenging—treasure he'd ever had. He planned to take his responsibility for their well-being *very* seriously.

Other than the mice and his second-grade class hamster, there was only one other time in Herb's life when he'd been entrusted with the care of a living thing. Herb had just started kindergarten when Mom got sick. His teacher that year had told him, nearly every day, that she was praying for their family. She'd also told him that if *he* prayed hard enough, and took good care of Mom and loved her and hugged her as much as he could, that he was doing his most important job. When she'd said that, Herb had thought that what she was telling him was: he had the power to make Mom better.

So he had done all the things Ms. Cheney had told him to do, and more, but Mom had died anyway. Herb had failed.

Since then, he'd vowed to take better care of everything that came into his possession. He wouldn't let anyone or anything else go. Now, he had his chance to prove he could take care of something all on his own. It was Herb's solemn duty to protect three little mice, and he couldn't wait to show everyone that he was responsible enough to live up to the task.

That afternoon, when Herb's dad pulled their big peach food truck into the campground where they would be staying that first night of their summer adventure, Herb set to work making his mice feel just as comfortable and cared for as the rest of the family. He had decorated their glass tank with a map, so the mice could see where they were traveling and feel like they were part of the family's adventure, too.

But Herb knew that *seeing* and *hearing about* an adventure wasn't the same as *having* an adventure. So while Freddy set up their two tents and Lucy got dinner ready, Herb transferred his mice from their glass enclosure into a lighter cardboard box, and brought them outside for some fresh air. He dropped snacks into the box and watched his tiny friends sniff and snuff the fresh, crisp air.

Once the tents were set up, Herb carried his mice

into the yellow tent he would be sharing with Dad. He set up his own sleeping bag, and then got the mice settled in at the foot of his little bed. He tucked one of his T-shirts into a corner of the box so that they would have something soft to sleep in for the night.

Just as soon as they were snuggly, Dad's voice echoed from somewhere outside the tent. "Kids! Time to bake!"

Herb scrambled to the tent's front flap and unzipped it. Dad had promised to teach them all how to make pie today, so they would have their first round of treats ready to sell the very next day in downtown Minneapolis. Herb was excited to help.

"Naptime," he told his mice. Then he blew them a kiss and zipped the tent up tight.

He scurried over to the food truck and hopped into the gleaming silver space. Dad was already busy measuring out flour and butter for the crusts. Lucy and Freddy tumbled into the truck behind Herb. "Wash up, then let's get this show on the road," he instructed. Herb did as he was told.

The four Peaches had decided as a group that their food truck's signature item would be Great Aunt Lucinda's famous peach pie. When Herb first saw Dad making this pie, he thought it looked pretty slimy: the peach slices Dad used were mushy and smushy, and the filling looked slimy and barfy when the peaches got all mixed up with sugar and cinnamon in the bowl. But after he saw and tasted the final product, he decided it was pretty cool how that mess of peaches could get turned into something so beautiful and perfect inside the food truck.

To figure out the rest of their pie offerings, Freddy had done some market research and told the family that selling some type of apple pie out of the truck was a must. A chocolate cream pie would also be a good addition, Lucy had pointed out, and Herb said that lemon meringue pie tasted like summer. To keep things exciting, Freddy thought they should test out some new recipes and add a special-feature pie or two into their rotation when things were going well.

"If we want to make real money," Dad said, wiping his flour-covered hands on his bright yellow apron, "we need to sell a lot of slices of pie."

"Duh," Lucy muttered under her breath. Herb wrapped his arm around her, since it seemed like she could use a hug.

"To sell a lot of slices," Dad went on, "we need to *make* a lot of pies. Which means everyone has to help with the baking each day."

Dad taped Great Aunt Lucinda's recipe card to the wall of the food truck and began his lesson. "Creating a perfect crust for your pie isn't as easy as it looks," he

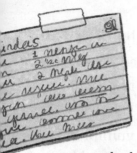

explained, as they each prepared a bowl full of crust ingredients. "It's an art form, really."

Herb gazed into his bowl as he mushed all the stuff together. He tried to think about his crust as art. It did remind him a little of the homemade play dough Lucy made for him sometimes. But this dough was crumbly and chunky and looked nothing like it was supposed to. He glanced over at his sister's crust. Lucy had finished mixing and was now rolling her crust out on one of the shiny counters. It looked paper-thin in some spots, chewy-thick in others, and the round of dough ripped in half when she tried to lower it into her pie tin. Herb knew his brilliant, perfect sister wasn't used to failing, but her crust experiment seemed to be a full-blown disaster.

Herb's big brother didn't seem to be faring any better. Every time Freddy tried to roll his dough into a flat disk, the whole pile of ingredients crumbled into buttery bits. Freddy finally gave up and started pressing pieces of his dough into the bottom of his pan, clearly hoping it would hold together after it was baked. The pan looked like a patchwork quilt of pressed-together dough. Freddy continued to pound at his crust dough, slamming his fist into the bottom of the pan to flatten and even it all out.

"Maybe we'd be better off buying ready-made crusts," Lucy suggested. "It would be a lot easier."

After trying and failing many times, Herb gave up on rolling out his crust the regular way. Instead, he was forming it into little balls that he then rolled in a sugar and cinnamon mixture. "Herb's Cinnaballs!" he cried, holding one up proudly. "Like donut holes, but yummier."

"Buy ready-made crust?" Dad scoffed, ignoring Herb. "Nonsense. That would be like buying a Pepperidge Farm cake from the grocery store and then selling it by the slice. Or buying McDonald's burgers and putting them in your own wrappers. This family specializes in *Peach* creations, not other people's stuff." He gestured at the lumpy crusts on the counter. "We have the power to turn this mess into something truly delicious and beautiful."

"But Pepperidge Farm cake is delicious," Freddy blurted. He looked around at his family's baking efforts. "And our homemade crusts look like—"

Dad cut him off. "Our crusts look like a first effort," he said. "Practice makes perfect. If Mom's team had given up on the solar window cling invention after their first effort, they never would have succeeded. Then we wouldn't have gotten the chance to set off on this family adventure." He pressed his own nearly perfect crust into a pan. "It's worth spending a little extra time on the things that matter."

Lucy snorted and shaped her dough into a ball again.

"Like homemade crust?" she asked as she slammed the ball down on the counter and began to roll it out again. "That's one of the things that matters most?"

"Obviously," Dad answered. "A good crust is the cornerstone of the Great Peach Experiment. The foundation we must build on!"

"Obviously," Lucy echoed. "When life gives you lemons," she muttered, so quietly only Herb could hear, "make peach pie. That makes perfect sense."

Herb grinned and thrust his pie tin full of dough balls toward his sister. "Can I interest you in one of Herb's Cinnaballs?"

THE MIDWEST

9

PEOPLE-WATCHING

Freddy loved sleeping in tents. He liked having nothing more than a thin swatch of fabric separating him and his bed from the outside world. He also liked the way you could open the screened sides of a tent and let a gentle breeze settle over you while you slept surrounded by the natural world (or, in his limited travel experience, surrounded by the backyard).

But as the Peach family tucked into their campground on that first night, Freddy quickly realized that tent camping in an RV- and food truck–friendly campground was *not* the same thing as tent camping in nature or their backyard. This summer's adventure was not shaping up to be *quite* what he'd expected . . . but he was certain it would be exciting in a different kind of way.

Because they'd driven into the campground in a food

truck, the only spot the Peaches were permitted to set up was a big, dirt-crusted space right next to the bustling bathroom building. Which meant people walked past—and through—their campsite all evening long.

Freddy didn't mind the lack of privacy. He discovered that people-watching in campgrounds was *much* better than most other places. There were campers with fun accents, quiet couples with yippy little dogs, old people who talked to themselves, chatty folks who talked to anyone who would listen, and one person who had decided it was entirely appropriate to wear nothing but a towel to travel from their own campsite to the showers!

Lucy had read Freddy and Herb a book called *Harriet the Spy* the previous summer, and in that story, Harriet liked to take notes about people she met and saw out in the world every day. Since then, Freddy had started sketching the people and things he saw in the world—it was more fun than writing stuff in a journal, and he liked to practice drawing people. Campgrounds were going to give him a lot of good material!

The plan was that Freddy and Lucy would share one tent for the summer, while Dad and Herb shared another. Freddy had insisted on this setup, since he was secretly terrified of Herb's mice (he was certain the wormy little critters would turn into vampire mice at night and eat him alive). Also, their dad snored. Even though she could sometimes be a little bossy, Freddy had decided Lucy was the best possible tent companion.

When they got to the campground, Freddy set up the tents, since he was the only one who'd assembled one before. Once the outer shell was in place, he and Lucy made the inside of their house-for-the-night look comfortable and cozy.

After their first, disastrous pie-making lesson in the food truck, they gobbled down a quick dinner, and then it was already time for bed. Dad told them all to get a good night's sleep, since they had a lot of work to do in the morning if they wanted to stay on schedule. They had to roll and bake crusts, and make all the pie fillings, first thing in the morning, so they would have *something* to sell during their first official day in business.

All three kids brushed their teeth in the big building beside their campsite, and then put on pj's. After, Herb joined his siblings in their tent so Lucy could read him his usual nighttime story. Freddy put on his headlamp and sketched while Lucy read aloud from *The*

Penderwicks. As soon as the chapter was finished, Herb yawned and sleepily shuffled off to his tent.

Freddy switched off his headlamp, listening to the sounds of the world around them—laughter from the group a few campsites over, some sort of bird or beast yip-yipping in a tree, the door of the bathroom swinging open and shut, Dad's not-so-gentle snoring pouring out of the neighboring tent, and the soft swish of Lucy turning pages in the book she was reading to herself. Freddy wasn't sure how much time passed before his eyes fluttered closed and his body fell into a deep, relaxed sleep filled with dreams of pie.

🥧 🥧 🥧

The next morning, Freddy woke early as the campground came alive around them. The tent provided no protection from the sounds of other campers waking and hustling to the bathrooms, shouting greetings to each other. Rain pattered on the fabric of the tent and bounced in noisy pings off the roof of the bathroom building. Dad had told them they'd be staying just outside Minneapolis for several nights, so Freddy didn't need to take the tents down or do any other chores to pack up. They just needed to bake a few good-looking pies, and then it would be time to head out for the first day of the Great Peach Experiment!

The morning got off to a hurried start. The kids all gobbled down a quick bowl of cereal under a tarp that Lucy had hung over the campsite's picnic table, then Freddy and Lucy joined Dad in the food truck to roll out more dough for crust and mix together some of the fillings. Dad had decided they should blind bake all of their crusts, which—Freddy had learned—meant that they would bake them before filling them. Dad said this helped keep the crust from getting soggy.

By the time they had finished their first crust-making lesson the night before, it was too late to turn on the food truck's generator and bake anything. Besides, all their first crusts had looked terrible. So Dad had gotten up early and mixed up another big batch of dough before breakfast. By eight o'clock, there was a ton of dough waiting to be rolled out and baked—and then, finally, it would be time to fill their first day's pies.

While his siblings helped to prepare pie, Herb had chosen to stay in his and Dad's tent and set up obstacle courses for his mice. He'd argued that they needed lots of company and exploration time now, because they would be alone for most of the rest of the day. As long as *Freddy* wasn't expected to look at or touch the mice (he wanted nothing to do with any kind of creature whose teeth *never stopped growing*!), he was fine with Herb bailing.

Besides, Dad said Herb was too little to do much baking anyway, so it didn't make a whole lot of sense for him to stand around doing nothing all morning. Sometimes, Freddy had noticed, Dad underestimated Herb. Though he was the youngest member of the family, Herb was bright and motivated and almost always willing to do just about anything. Hopefully their dad would notice that as the summer went on.

As soon as all the crust dough was rolled out and ready, Dad slid the pans into the food truck's ovens and then they began getting dressed and ready for their big day. Freddy could already tell this summer was going to be a vast improvement from the one he'd been dreading. They were on the road, exploring the country, spending time together as a family. His dad seemed relaxed and happy. Freddy knew this was exactly the kind of adventure the Peaches needed.

His only regret was that Mom couldn't be there to lead them. Opening a food truck and traveling had been *her* dream, and Freddy hated that she had never gotten a chance to do anything like this herself. Because of that, he desperately wanted this summer to go well, for Mom. Their brilliant and creative mother had experimented with and invented so many things during her life, but she hadn't ever gotten to celebrate any of them becoming truly successful. But now, Freddy had a chance to turn some of the money from her first successful invention into yet *another* success—and he had every intention of making that happen. He would make his mother proud. If they could make enough money and win the Food Truck Festival, it would be even better than a report card filled with straight As. It would change everything.

Freddy was whistling happily as he hustled back to the campsite from the bathroom, but his mouth froze in a pucker when he saw a thin wisp of smoke slithering out of the food truck's half-open back door. The crusts had only been in the oven for ten minutes. He ran toward the food truck, calling for his dad. Lucy responded first; she jumped out of the tent and grabbed a fire extinguisher from the cab of the food truck. She and Freddy covered their mouths and noses to keep from inhaling smoke as they crawled inside the truck.

There were no flames, but obviously something was very wrong. The ovens were belching out smoke, and the whole truck was filled with the smell of burned butter. Lucy held up the fire extinguisher, just in case, while Freddy turned off the ovens.

A few minutes later, once the smoke had cleared, the Peach family gathered around as Dad opened the ovens to assess the damage. "Looks like I got the time and temperature wrong," Dad said, scratching his head.

Every single one of their crusts was burned to a crisp.

"That's three hundred dollars worth of pie," Freddy groaned. "Up in smoke."

HERB'S CINNABALLS RECIPE

1. Wash your hands.
2. Get a clump of leftover crust dough.
3. Roll it into a ball.
4. Plop it in cinnamon-and-sugar mix.
5. Get an adult or Lucy to bake it
   (don't let it burn!).
6. Let it cool and enjoy. Yum yum!

From the Sketchbook of Freddy Peach:
HOW TO SPEND A MILLION DOLLARS

When I'm a rich guy, I know how I'll travel. There will
be no plain old food trucks for me. I'll get a private jet
and take the whole fifth-grade class on an epic field
trip where we stay in a fancy hotel with room service
and a pool in every room!

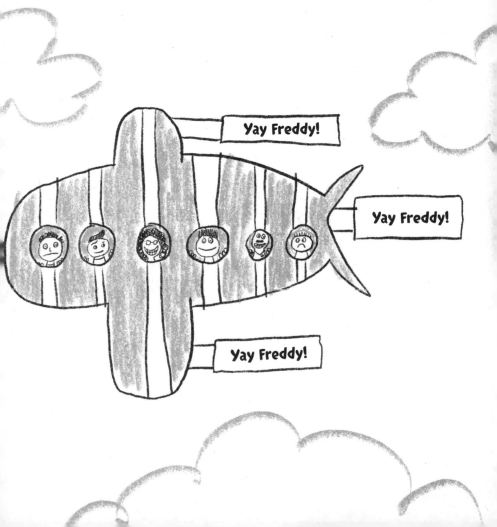

10

PEACH POWER

Lucy looked up from her book as her brothers raced toward the family's campsite later that evening. Herb was clutching two leashes in his hand. There was a small, yappy dog attached to the end of each.

"Where'd you get those dogs?" Lucy asked, bending down to scratch the fluffier of the two pups behind the ear. The dog skittered away from her and hid behind Herb. Herb scooped the little pup up into his arms and kissed it on the top of its head.

"The lady three campsites down let me borrow them," Herb explained.

Lucy gave him a warning look. *"Borrow,"* she told her littlest brother. "That doesn't mean *keep.*"

"I *know*," Herb said, rolling his eyes. "I don't *want* to keep them." Lucy noticed that he wouldn't look at her when he said that—because she knew as well as anyone that Herb never wanted to give up *anything* once he'd fallen in love with it. "Don't worry, Lucy. I just started a little dog-walking business."

"You started a business?" Lucy said, laughing.

"There's no *biz* in *business* unless you're making money," Freddy helpfully pointed out.

"Whatever." Herb sighed. "I started a dog-walking *volunteer*-ness. That's a kind of business where you don't make money."

"Kinda like our food truck," Lucy muttered.

"Hey, now," Freddy said, plunking down on the bench next to her. The second dog pawed at Freddy's leg, ignoring Lucy entirely. Herb bent down and clumsily picked it up in one arm, plunking the little pup—and its leash—onto Freddy's lap. Then Herb wandered off with the fluffy dog cradled in his arms, cooing into its floppy ear. Freddy quietly asked, "You're not giving up already, are you, Lu?"

Lucy shrugged. "What's the point? We're not cut out for this." She was pretty sure she wasn't the only member of the family who was already tempted to quit. Less than a week had passed since the food truck had landed in their driveway; just a few measly days, really, since Dad had surprised them with the million-dollar news, dropped his big summer-trip bomb, and set up this experiment.

They hadn't yet sold a single slice of pie, but Dad already looked weary and miserable, and he was constantly checking his phone to see if anyone at the university needed anything from him. Herb seemed bored and fidgety. Lucy was frustrated and annoyed. Miraculously, Freddy still seemed optimistic, even though it was abundantly clear this experiment was going to be a miserable failure.

They had worked their butts off and burned or ruined hundreds of dollars' worth of ingredients without selling a single slice of pie. They'd eaten hot dogs for three out of the last four meals. Herb had let his mice crawl *into* the peanut butter jar that afternoon, making the rest inedible to humans. Lucy and Freddy's tent had sprung a leak, so her pillow was damp and her book soaked. To top it all off, the campground bathroom had run out of toilet paper.

That evening, while their dad prepared a fresh batch of dough and her brothers explored the campground, Lucy had been sitting under their rain-soaked tarp, pretending to read while secretly stewing. Her book was open, but whenever she tried to make out the words, they swam and wobbled out of focus.

Lucy was angry with herself for getting so upset. It

wasn't like any of this really mattered; the whole summer was just a bad idea: a short-lived experiment to pretend they were still the kind of family who did fun things together.

"So we burned a few pies," Freddy said as Lucy folded the top corner of her page to mark her spot. "It's not the end of the world."

"I know you've done the same research I have," Lucy said. Freddy wasn't stupid, even though he sometimes thought he was. He had a mind for business, and he knew more facts about more things than anyone else Lucy had ever met. "It's not easy to make money running a food truck. We're doomed to fail."

"It's not *only* about money," Freddy said. "We can have fun *trying* to succeed."

"It's a waste of mom's hard-earned cash," Lucy said. "And our time." She had tried to convince herself that this time could be different; because they had embarked on this experiment for Mom, it changed everything. But remembering Mom didn't help. It just made her wonder what this whole experience would be like if Mom were actually *there*. The bottom line was, *nothing* had worked right since she died.

"So, maybe this experiment *is* a waste of money and time," Freddy agreed. "But part of the fun of creating new stuff is messing up and then figuring out how to improve for the next time. Do you remember how Mom used to say, if you want to build something incredible, you have to keep trying, even when everything seems like it's falling apart?" He lifted his eyebrows, obviously waiting for Lucy to reply.

Lucy huffed. Mom *had* said that—a lot. And Lucy herself had encouraged her brothers to heed that advice many times over the past few years. It was easy to give up and quit when things didn't go according to plan, but Mom had always said that no great thing ever came out of a first try.

Freddy held the dog in front of Lucy's face and waved its little paw at her. Then, in a funny voice, he said, "We've made our first mistake, and now we know we have to keep closer watch on the ovens to make sure we're baking things at the right temp for the right amount of time. That's not a mistake we'll make again."

Lucy laughed. "I guess that's true."

"The four of us are going to have plenty of challenges and problems along the way," Freddy told her, standing up. "But with three smart Peaches—and my good looks—we can handle anything. Right?"

Herb came racing back over, his little doggie pal leading the way. "Dad needs help in the food truck," he announced, plunking down next to Lucy on the picnic bench. "He can't open the new bag of flour."

Lucy lifted one eyebrow in Freddy's direction. "We can handle anything, huh?"

Freddy laughed. But then he grew serious, and stood before his siblings to announce, "Here's the thing, you guys. I've been thinking about what Dad said last weekend: that once upon a time, he and Mom had all these dreams they never got to go after. Now, Mom's invention drops this huge chunk of money on us and look how Dad chose to use part of it: to spend time with us, doing something Mom wanted us all to do together."

When Freddy said this, Lucy cringed. She'd chosen to respect her dad's wishes and not tell her brothers that he had been *forced* to take time off work. It would just disappoint them if they knew the truth, and they were obviously going to need Freddy's optimism and Herb's hopefulness if the family wanted to have any chance of surviving this summer.

Freddy went on, "Dad *could* have taken all that cash and used it to pay off the house, or go to another work conference, or sock it all away in his retirement savings—but he didn't. He's investing part of it in us *now*. Which means this time together must matter to him, right? If we can show him that we can do a good job with this, maybe . . ."

Freddy didn't need to finish the sentence. Lucy and

Herb knew what he was going to say: that if the Peach Pie Truck *were* a success, maybe things *could* change.

Herb nodded. "But what actually makes a food truck successful?" he asked. "How will we *know*?"

"We need to make money, obviously," Freddy said, rubbing the little dog's ear like a good-luck charm. "Dad said if we make ten thousand bucks, and win the Ohio Food Truck Festival, that's success. If we can do that, we'll prove to Dad that it was worth it for him to take all this time off. But if we *don't* succeed, we're going to lose him to work again. Probably for good." He set the dog gently on the ground and took a deep breath. "Lucy, I know you're not super-excited about this whole plan, but don't forget that Dad's *trying* to share with us something that mattered to Mom. We all have to decide if we want to help it succeed or watch it fail. I personally think it's worth a shot to try to succeed."

Herb nodded solemnly. "Definitely worth it."

For a long moment, Lucy said nothing. She was still skeptical, but Freddy had made a good point. "Okay."

Freddy pumped his fist and whooped, which elicited a little yip and nervous barking from the pup at his feet. "Let's make a promise to go all-in—for Mom—okay?" He glanced at Lucy. "And for us." He held out his hand, palm down, in front of his two siblings. "Pile up,

Peaches," he ordered. Herb slapped his hand on top of Freddy's. Lucy wrapped her hand around both Freddy's and Herb's and squeezed. With a big smile, Freddy said, "We're in this together."

"Together," Lucy and Herb agreed.

Freddy grinned. "Peach power!"

Dear Great Aunt Lucinda,

We made it to Minneapolis. My tent leaks, Freddy's scared of Herb's mice (he thinks they're going to turn into vampire mice and eat him in the night—ha!), and we burned all our pies. So things are going really well! I'm trying to have fun, I promise. It's nice spending time with my brothers and Dad doing stuff together. But I'm nervous this experiment is going to end like all of Dad's other promises. (Remember when he borrowed all that camping stuff from you, so we could go to the Boundary Waters for a week last summer? We're finally using the tents for the first time on this trip.) The second things go bad, he's going to give up and I'll have to figure out an escape plan. I don't WANT that to happen, but it will. And Herb and Freddy will be crushed.

Love,
Lucy

PS: Herb met a couple dogs at our campground that would fit in perfectly with your pack!

11

PEACH SHORTAGE

On Wednesday morning, with Freddy overseeing every step of the process, the family managed to make six decent-looking pies—two apple, two slightly runny French silk, and two lopsided lemon meringue. Dad offered to be in charge of monitoring the peach pies while they baked and the kids all showered—but he got distracted reading a science article he'd pulled up on his phone, and all four of the family's signature pies burned.

But six pies were better than none, so the family set off to a busy downtown Minneapolis street for their first day in business.

When they arrived, a dozen other food trucks had already set up shop for the day. It was still raining—a weak but constant drizzle—so no one was really out and about looking for food. Freddy decided the slow, rainy morning was a good opportunity to do a little research on some of the other food trucks and maybe check out their business plans. He let the rest of the family get things set up while he grabbed an umbrella and headed out to charm his way into some useful information. Taking inspiration from other artists always helped Freddy with his own art projects, and hopefully this approach would help him in business, too.

The food truck parked directly next to theirs was called Hola Arepa, and it sold a bunch of delicious-looking meats and veggies served in soft little masa corn cake pockets. It was the only truck that had a line of customers, and Freddy decided the staff of that truck probably wouldn't be willing to chat with him unless he was standing in line to buy something. Maybe he'd come back for lunch, but he wasn't hungry yet.

Next to Hola Arepa was a truck selling fancy juices—for nine dollars apiece! "That's insane," Freddy muttered. "Who buys juice for nine bucks?" Just as he said it, a group of middle-aged ladies ran through the rain and ducked under the juice truck's canopy. They all ordered not one, but *two* juices each! "Some people are crazy," Freddy announced.

He passed a tiny pizza truck, a fancy-looking taco truck, and a huge blue-and-black food truck that had a whole variety of items made with tater tots. He jotted them all down and drew a picture of each truck in his sketchbook. He decided it would be fun to design his dream food truck later, when they got back to their campsite.

Toward the end of the food truck lineup, Freddy came upon a truck selling crepes. Their menu boasted ham-and-Swiss-cheese crepes, mushroom crepes, and two sweet crepes: chocolate banana and sugar butter. Sweet crepes were similar enough to pie that Freddy felt this was the best place to do a little investigating. Time for more research! He would do whatever he could to make himself useful to the family business. Even if he wasn't good at math and money stuff, he knew he could figure out ways to help their experiment succeed.

The girl staffing the crepe truck looked like she was somewhere between high school and parent age, and she seemed bored out of her mind. Freddy sauntered over and said hello. "We're new here," he explained, in his best take-me-seriously voice. "Actually, we're new to the food truck business. Do you happen to have any tips for us? Business owner to business owner?"

"Are you for real?" The girl laughed, then stood up

and rubbed her hands on her apron. "Do you want a crepe, hon?"

Freddy pulled his eyebrows together. "No, I don't want a crepe. I'm with the Peach Pie Truck." He gestured with his thumb, pointing toward the end of the line of colorful trucks. "And I was hoping to ask you a few questions about how you run your business. Successes, failures, best practices. Fun facts, tips, what have you."

"You're adorable," the girl said.

Freddy scowled. *Adorable* described a puppy, or a fluffy baby panda, or three-year-old Herb in the bath with a sudsy bubble beard. *Adorable* did not get taken seriously. "How often do you buy supplies for your truck?" Freddy asked, ignoring the girl's unintentional dig. "Daily, weekly, or on an as-needed basis?"

"Me?" the girl said, frowning. "I don't buy anything. I just show up and work here. Summer job."

Freddy rolled his eyes. This interview was a waste of time. The Internet had been a better source of facts than crepe girl. With a winning smile, Freddy saluted her, and said, "Good to know. Thanks for all your helpful tips. Have a nice afternoon." Then he sauntered back to the Peach Pie Truck, hoping to see people queued up for pie. But all he saw was Herb, drawing curlicues on the corner of the chalkboard menu they'd affixed to the side of the truck. Their three pies were listed on the board:

Apple Crumb Pie . . . $5
Lemon Meringue Pie . . . $5
French Silk Pie . . . $5

They hadn't yet bought ice cream, so they couldn't offer the apple pie à la mode. But it wasn't that hot today, so who wanted ice cream anyway?

As Freddy approached, Herb wrote:

Herb's Cinnaballs . . . $2

on the bottom of the menu. Freddy was tempted to walk over and smudge it out with his fist. But he decided it couldn't hurt to let Herb try to sell his weird little crust balls. Any sale was better than no sale at all.

Freddy scanned the sidewalk, wondering where all the customers were. It was after noon, and they should have had *some* business by now! He'd noticed that crowds tended to draw people's attention, so he decided he'd try to figure out some way to look busy so people would think their truck was popular.

"Herb," he whispered, "pretend you're in line."

"Why?" Herb asked. "I don't want pie. Pie is the pits."

"We're creating demand," he explained to his brother. "Trust me." Then he went inside the truck and told Dad to come outside to stand in line, too. Once Herb, Freddy, and Dad were all in line, Freddy said, "Lucy, you pretend to serve us."

"This is craz—" Lucy began, laughing. But she quieted down when she saw a group of guys making their way toward the Peach Pie Truck's fake line.

Freddy shot her a look that said, *See?*

The three guys chatted with one another as they stood at the back of the "line." Freddy turned to them, and said, "I'm still deciding what I want. You can cut in front of me. All these pies look top-notch, so it's hard to choose!"

"Yes, um, same here," Dad said, looking uncomfortable as he stepped aside. He clearly wasn't good at pretending, but the fake line strategy had worked. Dad mumbled, "You can, uh, hop ahead of me, too."

"I don't like pie," Herb announced, which made the guys laugh.

"Okay," one of them said, scanning the menu. Then he rubbed his hands together and told Lucy, "I'll get a slice of peach pie, please."

"Make that two," his friend said.

"I'll go with apple," the third chimed in.

"I'm so sorry," Lucy said, flustered. She glanced at Freddy, for once looking desperate for help. "We don't have peach today, we, uh—"

Freddy spoke up, trying to cover for his sister. "Yeah, I read in the paper that there was a—um—a peach shortage this week. The whole Midwest had trouble with their shipment from, uh, bluh bluh bluh." He mumbled something no one could understand, and then trailed off.

"Weird," one of the peach pie fans said, turning around to look at Lucy again. "Okay, then, I guess I'll get apple, too."

"I'll go with lemon meringue," the third said. "Too bad about the peach thing, since that's the name of your truck. Must be rough."

"Yeah," Lucy said, glancing at Freddy with a helpless shrug. She handed the guys their slices of pie, then passed each a fork. "That's five dollars apiece."

They all paid, and Freddy felt a flutter of excitement in the pit of his belly. Their first sales! It felt *great.* "Enjoy!" Freddy cried out, waving as the guys walked away. "The Peach Pie Truck will be here tomorrow, too, so tell all your friends to stop by."

As soon as their customers were out of hearing range, the Peaches whooped and hugged.

"Three slices sold," Freddy cheered. "We're on a roll here, people. *A roll!*"

From the Sketchbook of Freddy Peach:
CHERRY IN A SPOON

Today we saw Spoonbridge and Cherry, a really cool sculpture in Minneapolis that's made out of aluminum and stainless steel. Fun fact: it weighs 7,000 pounds! Maybe one of my art installations will be on display at this sculpture garden someday.

PEACH!
(not a cherry)

MINNEAPOLIS MONEY:
(BY HERB)

* Cost of Pie Supplies: $632
* Sales: $70
* Total Profit: -$562

12

MOVING ON

After a couple long, wet days in Minneapolis—and only *two* where they'd actually had pies to sell—Dad decided it was time to move on to drier, pie-friendlier pastures. "I'd say it's time to hit the road," he announced after they closed up the truck on Thursday afternoon. "It's important to know when to cut your losses, and I'd say the Minneapolis leg of our journey has been a total bust."

Holding a half-empty cup of coffee in one hand, Dad led Herb and his siblings toward the nearby coffee shop that had let the Peaches use their restroom all day (as long as Dad kept buying fresh cups of coffee). "Seems like Minneapolis is not our lucky spot. We've had a crummy go of it here, but maybe we'll fare better in Chicago."

Herb didn't think Minneapolis had been even a little

bit crummy. It had been a rough start, and they hadn't sold a lot of pie, but they'd had some fun adventures. And to tell the truth, Herb didn't care *where* they went next—as long as he was with his family, he got to sleep in a tent again, his mice were happy and healthy, and there was water to swim in.

So far, Herb had managed to meet his personal summer goal of swimming every day. The big, crowded campground just outside Minneapolis wasn't anything special, but Herb had made a couple of wonderful dog friends that he was going to miss a lot after they left!

He'd also started a new collection on the road— he'd begun gathering empty toilet paper rolls from the campground bathroom (there were a *lot* of them!) and storing them under his seat in the truck. He was pretty sure they would come in handy for something, someday.

Their Minneapolis campground had been close to both the Mississippi River *and* the St. Croix River. Each morning, Dad had stopped the food truck so Herb could wade in a different river each day. The water had been too chilly for him to duck his head under, but he'd splashed around near shore and kicked water at his siblings, and Dad had finally taught him how to skip a flat, round stone across the surface of the swollen, rain-flooded river (Herb had been trying to master that for years back home, on Lake Superior).

Then, that morning, after they'd finished baking their pies and loaded up the truck, Lucy had begged Dad to stop at a big, beautiful flower garden she'd heard about from her best friend, Maren. There was a short break in the rain, and it felt good to play outside. While Freddy sketched bugs and Dad fretted over some of the work he'd brought along on the trip, Lucy and Herb set off on a walk together. They found a rocky waterfall fountain that Herb was allowed to splash around in. He wasn't sure the fountain officially counted as *swimming*, but it had been fun nonetheless.

Minneapolis was big and exciting and full of neat stuff. They had even found a *huge* sculpture of a giant cherry sitting on a spoon. Dad had pulled the food truck over to the side of a busy road and idled in a loading zone so Freddy could hop out quick to sketch it.

Now, after several full days of fun adventures (but crummy pie sales), Herb skipped along beside Dad as they made their way toward the coffee shop toilet. Dad wrapped his arm around Herb's shoulder. Herb nuzzled in close, letting his dad squeeze him tighter than felt comfortable. Dad didn't pull him close like this very often, and it felt good to walk down a strange street in an unfamiliar city under his father's arm. Herb's siblings traipsed along behind them, and Freddy was chatting his sister's ear off, which meant Herb and his dad could enjoy a few special, one-on-one minutes. He gazed up at Dad, and said, "I love you, Dad. Thanks for taking us on this trip and letting me collect all these fun new memories. And for letting me swim every day."

His dad blinked, then a huge smile took over his face. "I love you, too, Herbie."

"Dad?" Herb asked a few moments later, when he noticed Dad had tears on his cheeks. "Are you crying because we didn't sell very many pies in Minneapolis? We still have lots of time to make more money before the Ohio Food Truck Festival."

His dad laughed. "I'm not too worried about that yet. I'm actually feeling happy. I don't know why I'm crying. It doesn't make much sense, does it?"

"Lucy says you're allowed to cry for lots of reasons," Herb told him. "Sometimes I cry when I'm scared at night, but then she gives me her duck to sleep with and that helps. And one time I saw a dead squirrel mashed up in the road—that made me cry, especially when the crows started pecking at it and then there were brains and guts and stuff smeared all over. And last week, Andrew said we couldn't be friends when third grade starts because I decided to play tag with Ruby and Zubair during recess, instead of four square with him. But Lucy told me he would get over it, and she was right, because now we're friends again."

His dad nodded. "Lucy is a very good sister, isn't she?"

"She's the best," Herb agreed. "Don't tell anyone else, but she's my favorite family."

🐾 🐾 🐾

The Peaches drove out of downtown Minneapolis in the middle of rush hour traffic. The rain made it impossible for them to open windows, which meant it felt like an oven inside the cab. But Herb didn't care. His dad had given each of the kids fifty dollars to spend on souvenirs during the trip, and Herb had already spent five of his on a little handheld fan he'd spotted at a gas station (and immediately knew he needed). After relaxing in the fan's breeze for a few moments, he turned it on his mice, knowing they would probably appreciate a little fresh air, too. But when the blast from the fan hit the little critters, all three of them dove for cover under their T-shirt bed, so Herb turned the fan back on himself. He smirked at Freddy, then kicked up his feet and luxuriated in the cool air. Herb knew his brother was probably jealous of his very smart purchase.

At every gas station they stopped at (and they had to stop often!), Herb shopped around for more treasures like the fan. There were so many things he'd seen that he desperately wanted to add to his collection. But he was trying to save some of his money, feeling certain he'd *feel* it when he spotted the exact right thing to buy.

Every time they stopped for gas, he also begged his dad to buy one of those scratch-off lottery tickets. But no matter how many times he asked, Dad firmly refused. "A waste of money," he said. "No one ever wins those things. You'd be better off throwing a bunch of coins from a bridge and wishing for a million bucks to land in your lap."

Herb pointed out that they *definitely* wouldn't ever win the lottery if they didn't ever *buy* a scratch-off card, but this logic never changed Dad's mind. Lucy grumbled that it was insane that Dad believed opening a food truck (without any experience running a business like that) was a sensible use of money, but he thought buying *lottery tickets* was wasteful. "From what I can tell, both the lottery and this food truck require a huge amount of luck," she muttered, just loud enough for Herb to hear. Then even more quietly, she added, "And luck is something this family definitely doesn't have a lot of."

Shortly after they got out of the worst of the

Minneapolis traffic, the food truck rumbled over a long bridge out of Minnesota and into Wisconsin, then headed north. They were taking the long route to Chicago, because Freddy had begged to stop and see some sort of giant fish he'd read about. Freddy was convincing enough that Dad had reluctantly agreed to the detour.

They were in the truck for a little more than two hours before it was time to stop at the fish statue for dinner. Lucy had gone to a grocery store that afternoon and packed a picnic of BLT sandwiches and chopped salad. Herb was relieved to discover there was no pie in her dinner basket. Pie still made him feel icky, and just looking at it and smelling it every day was enough for him.

"Welcome to Hayward, Wisconsin," Freddy said, as they all tumbled out of the huge vehicle. "This fiberglass muskie is also the home of the Fresh Water Fishing Hall of Fame. It's four and a half stories tall, and as long as a Boeing 757. Pretty cool, huh?" He pulled out his sketchbook and began drawing a mutated version of the fish. Herb giggled as his brother drew huge teeth and horns, making the giant muskie look much more terrifying than it did in real life. At least, he *hoped* muskies didn't look like that in real life, or he'd have to remove lakes from his swimming goal. No way would he put his feet anywhere near a fish like that!

The rain had finally let up—for good, it seemed—so the family found a grassy space to set up their picnic. After just a few bites of her sandwich, Lucy lay back in the grass and disappeared inside her book. She had already finished both *A Night Divided* and *Amina's Voice*, and was now reading *Fish in a Tree*.

Seeing his sister with her book gave Herb an idea. He raced back to the food truck and grabbed his copy of *The Penderwicks*. This was the novel he and Lucy had been reading together, chapter by chapter, each night before bedtime. When he was lucky, she'd read him a chapter during the day, too. Now, he dropped it on his sister's belly and said, "Read?"

She muttered, "I'm reading my own book."

Herb pleaded, "Please? Then everyone can listen to the story. We just got to an exciting part, remember?"

Lucy reluctantly sat up and cradled *The Penderwicks* in her hands. Herb knew it was one of the books on Lucy's summer reading list, but he also knew she'd already read it three times before. One of the reasons Herb loved the story so much is that it was about a family of fun siblings and their really nice dad who have an exciting summer adventure together. Now that *his* family was on a similar adventure, Herb was enjoying the book even more.

"Are you two reading a book together?" Dad asked, holding out his hand for a look.

"Lucy reads me a chapter every night," Herb announced. "Sometimes I read a page to her, too, but Lucy has to help me with some of the hard words."

"You're reading novels already?" Dad asked, looking shocked.

Herb stuck out his chin proudly. "Yep. I'm a good reader."

"I see." Dad nodded. "How wonderful."

"Well?" Herb said, turning to Lucy. "Are you going to read to us or not?"

Dad clutched the book tighter in his hands. "Would it be okay if I read the next chapter? To everyone? Maybe we could do a *family* read-aloud this summer?"

Lucy and Herb exchanged a surprised look. Then Lucy shrugged her approval, while Herb flopped down on his belly and perched his chin on his hands. "I like the character Skye best," he told his dad. "I think you will, too."

"I see," Dad said again, opening the book to their folded-down page. Freddy continued to draw, while Lucy pulled out one of the LEGO three-in-one sets she'd packed for the trip. Dad stretched his legs out in front of him and cleared his throat. "Skye, huh? If she's your favorite, I can't wait to meet her."

KILLER MUSKIE

The giant muskie in Hayward, Wisconsin, was insane!

13

WORLD'S SMALLEST POOL

After their picnic, eaten in the shadow of Hayward's giant fiberglass fish (which, even Lucy had to admit, was pretty awe-inspiring), the Peaches got back on the road.

Dad suggested they push on through and drive all the way to Chicago that night, so they could get up and try to sell more pies the very next day. "We've got a lot of hard work ahead of us if we want to have any chance of winning the Food Truck Festival!" he explained. But there was a lot of cheering when, a few hours into the evening's drive, Dad yawned loudly and announced that he was too tired to drive any farther.

So the family stopped for the night between Minneapolis and Chicago, at a rural campground somewhere in the middle of Wisconsin. Though it was dark when they arrived, there was a sign at the campground entrance that promised an outdoor pool and a game room. Since it was long past bedtime, Lucy told Herb she would take him to the pool first thing in the morning.

As soon as they had their tents set up, Lucy stretched out inside her sleeping bag and tried to read, but she fell asleep with her book open almost as soon as her head hit the pillow. She slept soundly until morning, waking from a deep sleep when her little brother zipped open her tent and begged her to take him to the pool. Lucy consulted her watch and decided that eight o'clock was late enough. Herb had gone almost one whole week of summer break without stepping foot in a real pool, and if they'd been home, she would have taken him to the community center pool at least four times by now.

The three Peach kids changed into their swim-suits, stuffed Herb into a life jacket for extra safety, and followed a trail of rickety wooden signs to the camp-ground's outdoor pool. They left their Dad to drink his morning coffee and read his articles in peace. As they headed off, Dad called out, "Hustle back—we can't afford to waste time!" Lucy groaned inwardly, but flashed him a thumbs-up.

There was a big, thick iron fence around the pool, but the gate wasn't locked. Lucy pushed it open, and the Peaches got their first glimpse of the campground's "pool."

"Do you think we'll all fit into this puddle at the same time?" Freddy asked, laughing. "Or maybe we should take turns? I bet I could jump from one side of the pool to the other without actually landing in the water!" Then he added, "I think I saw a picture of this exact pool in *Guinness World Records,* under the category 'World's Smallest Pool.' "

Lucy giggled. "It's totally possible all the water in this pool will overflow if all three of us get in at the same time." Nevertheless, she tossed their towels onto the only chair that fit on the pool deck and dragged her big toe through the water. The pool was chilly, but the air was warm enough that she knew it wouldn't matter. "But I'm willing to risk it."

Herb was the only one who didn't seem at all fazed by the size of the pool. It was wider and deeper than a bathtub, and he didn't have to wash his hair while he played. Lucy knew that was all that mattered to him. "Incoming!" he howled, cannonballing in. Water sprayed in all directions, soaking his siblings. Herb bounced to the surface of the water, then bobbed up and down in the middle of the pool. If he reached his arms out as wide as they would go, he could almost touch both sides.

But a pool was a pool, and within just a few minutes, all three kids were floating and splashing and had made up a game involving a found Ping-Pong ball and one of Herb's life jacket straps. They could have played for hours, but not long after they got in, Dad appeared at the gate and told them it was time to hit the road.

"Just a few more minutes?" Herb begged. "Come in with us! It's fun."

Dad shook his head. "Time to go. There are people in Chicago who are waiting for pie, and we can't afford to dillydally!"

Freddy hopped out and shook the water out of his hair. A few seconds later, the other two dragged themselves out of the water and wrapped up in towels. Herb shuffled his feet as they followed their dad back to the campsite, his toes growing dustier and dirtier with each step.

"We'll swim again soon," Lucy whispered to him.

"Tomorrow for sure," Herb whispered back. "Dad promised we could swim every day. And a promise is a promise."

Lucy wrapped his little hand in hers. Dad's promises didn't always mean much. "I hope so." What she *didn't* want to tell her brother is that they would be driving right by Wisconsin Dells that very morning. Wisconsin Dells was, according to its website, "The Waterpark

Capital of the World"—and it was also Herb's dream vacation destination.

The previous afternoon, when she and her dad were out of her brothers' earshot, Lucy had suggested that perhaps they could stop at the Dells as a special treat. "We're really not in any rush," she reminded him. "It would be a bonus adventure. Something fun for us to do along the way. Isn't that an important part of this family experiment?"

"Nonsense," Dad had said, adjusting the brim of his big, dorky hat. "We have a schedule, and a game plan, and there simply isn't *time* to make day-long stops just on a whim. For an experiment to succeed, Lucy, you can't just drop everything willy-nilly when something better comes along. You've got to focus." He nodded resolutely. "We're trying to make a go of this food truck business, and we need to keep our eyes on the prize. We have a lot of work to do to prepare and perfect our business model if we're going to be ready for the Food Truck Festival in Ohio."

So Lucy dropped it. Though there had been a few moments during the past few days when Lucy had begun to wonder if maybe her dad *could* change and help figure out a new way to be as a family, conversations like this always reminded her of why she'd stopped trusting him several years ago. He could never be the parent her brothers so desperately wanted him to be, and it was her job to manage their expectations.

But then, just as they were loading up the last of their stuff and climbing into the truck to hit the road, Dad informed them that their route had changed. "I have a fun surprise," he said cheerily. Lucy felt a glimmer of hope. Dad went on, "We're going to be making a bonus stop on our route."

Did Dad have a change of heart? she wondered. *Is he actually making an effort to stop and do something* fun *as a family?* Lucy glanced at Herb; she was excited to see his reaction when he found out they'd be stopping at Wisconsin Dells to swim and ride waterslides all day. Maybe there was hope for this trip after all!

Dad went on, "I was able to pull some strings, and I have very good news. We are taking a detour, kids. Hold on to your hats, because we're going to be stopping for a few nights to sell some of our delicious pies in exciting, fun-filled Madison, Wisconsin!"

Herb—who'd been looking up at Dad like he was some kind of hero—cheered loudly at this news.

"Wait a second. We have time to take an unplanned detour because *you* want to," Lucy cried, lifting her eyebrows. "But not for *us*, for *fun*?" As far as she could tell, this detour did *not* sound exciting.

"What's so fun about Madison?" Herb asked hopefully, before Dad could answer Lucy's question.

Dad cleared his throat, and said proudly, "Good ol' Madison just so happens to be the city where I finished my undergraduate degree in geochemistry!"

Herb blinked. "Oh."

Lucy wanted to say, "See? Not exciting," but she held her tongue.

"It's also the second-largest city in Wisconsin," Freddy offered with a weak smile. "And I guess *this* is kind of an exciting fact: Madison's official city bird is a plastic pink flamingo. So, um . . . yay?"

Dad clapped him on the shoulder. "That's the spirit, Freddy-boy. That's. The. Spirit."

THE MIDWEST

From the Sketchbook of Freddy Peach:
HOW TO SPEND A MILLION DOLLARS

When I sell some of my art to the Minneapolis Sculpture Garden, I'm going to buy a private island and fill it with roller coasters, waterslides, hidden tunnels, and a bunch of weird, random sculptures: messy piles of socks, empty food boxes stacked up so they look like a massive Yoda, statues made out of dirty cans. Stuff like that.

Wish you were here!

Dear Aunt Lucinda,

Today we drove past Wisconsin Dells and Dad didn't stop. You can see EVERYTHING from the highway—waterslides, fountains, pools. It was torture. I tried to keep Herb distracted by doing card tricks while we went past, but it didn't work. He didn't miss a thing. Poor Herbie.

Random Q: Have you ever thrown a pie in someone's face? I've had to whip a lot of cream for pies lately, and I keep wondering what it would feel like to pie someone or get pied. I think it would feel kind of good—cold, smushy, and sweet. It's been hot, and the truck is always like a thousand degrees hotter than the world around it, so ANYTHING cold sounds pretty good to me.

Love,
Lucy

14

MUSIC FESTIVAL FINDS & FRIENDS

"This is it!" Freddy cheered early Saturday morning, as he whipped cream for the top of the turtle pies. "I can feel it. This is going to be the weekend we turn things around."

"Our pies do look pretty good," Lucy said. She stood next to the countertop filled with baked treats—apple crumb pie, Aunt Lucinda's peach pie, creamy turtle pie, and blueberry lattice pie. "This is the best batch yet."

Freddy agreed that their pies *looked* great. He also knew they *tasted* great. He had taken it upon himself to spoon out a little sample from each bowl of pie filling before it got wrapped up inside its crust that morning. Freddy felt this was a noble gesture and another important contribution to the family business. *Someone* had to taste the pies before they sold them to customers, and he was as good a candidate for that job as anyone. (Better than *Herb*, that was for sure. Herb actually *cried* when their dad threatened to make him eat more pie. Big wimp.)

When all their pies were prepared and tucked into the truck's coolers and cabinets for safe transport, the Peaches made their way to the giant, dusty vendor lot set up on the outskirts of the Midwest's Premier Blues Music Festival. As soon as they arrived, Freddy quickly scanned the other food trucks getting ready for a weekend of big business.

MIDWEST'S PREMIER BLUES MUSIC FESTIVAL

From where he stood, Freddy could see signs boasting hot dogs, cotton candy, Thai ice cream (which he would need to investigate further), barbecue, smoothies and salads, gyros, sushi (he wondered how they kept *that* fresh inside a metal truck on a hot day), Korean barbecue, Philly cheesesteaks, and the "World's Largest Sandwiches" (Freddy was certain this claim could not be true, since he had seen photos of the World's Largest Sandwich and it would not fit on any of the trucks in this lot). The air smelled like hot oil and french fries, and giant generators cooked up suffocating heat and unpleasant noises all around them.

Freddy loved everything about it: the people, the heat, the smells, the noise, the dirt, the hustle and bustle. It was *exciting*!

After helping his family get set up for their day of service and writing out their current menu on the chalkboard, Freddy wandered around getting to know a few of their food truck neighbors. Jim the cheesesteak guy was from Kenosha, Wisconsin, and he had recently become a vegetarian—which Freddy found fascinating for a guy who sold meat shavings on a roll. The Thai ice cream couple were apparently a bestselling vendor at the Minnesota State Fair—Freddy convinced them to do a product swap so he could try their delicious ice cream, which they made by pouring some ice-cream-batter-type stuff on a super-cold surface before scraping it into curly, creamy, frozen tubes. A burger truck—operated by a skinny lady named Aretha, who lived in Madison—sold big, stuffed burgers that made Freddy's mouth water. The food selection was incredible, unlike anything he had ever seen before.

But nothing—not even all that yummy food—could beat the people-watching. Every time Freddy got a break from working the counter in his family's truck, he wandered around the festival grounds sketching rough illustrations of some of the people he saw. The beards and mustaches on some of the guys were varied and interesting enough to fill dozens of pages in his sketchbook.

Freddy dared his brother to sneak up behind the *very* hairy guy they'd nicknamed the Yeti, touch his beard, and sneak away before the fellow noticed him. Freddy could tell Herb was tempted—he never liked to let dares go unanswered—but he took a pass and double-dared *Freddy* to do the same thing. Freddy got close but backed away at the last second. There were probably *things* living inside the Yeti's beard—possibly even a family of mice, and Freddy wasn't willing to risk it.

With so much to see, and so many hungry people swarming the food truck lot, the day passed quickly. Shortly after three o'clock, Dad declared, "We are sold out!"

"Everything?" Lucy asked, incredulous.

"We even sold three batches of Herb's Cinnaballs to that guy with an Abe Lincoln beard," Dad said.

"*Victory!*" Herb cried, raising his fist high and proud. "Herb's Cinnaballs for the win!"

"Nice," Lucy said, a huge smile on her face.

"Nice indeed," Dad agreed. He pulled his wide-brimmed hat off his head and mopped his brow with an orange bandanna.

Freddy was relieved that they'd finally had a good day of sales. He so badly wanted the Great Peach Experiment to be successful, and he loved seeing his family celebrate together. Tomorrow, he was sure, would be even better. They were on an upswing; he could *feel* it. Money was rolling in! "For tomorrow, I think we should make double the number of pies we sold today," he said eagerly. "In just four hours we sold every slice today—and it's still early. I think we could easily sell twice as many tomorrow. With the right number of pies, we could make some serious moola."

Dad nodded his agreement. "If we're going to do that, we'll have to divide and conquer on some of tonight's tasks. We need to stock up on supplies and ingredients, clean out the truck, and mix up a whole lot of fresh dough."

Freddy piped up. "Herb and I can work together to clean the truck and empty the tank." The gray water tank held each day's used water. Freddy found the process of emptying it fascinating, which was lucky, since both Dad and Lucy gagged when they had to handle that particular job. There was a surprising number of unappealing tasks that had to be done every day when you ran a food truck—cleaning, scrubbing, emptying disgusting things, picking up trash. Freddy *liked* all the weird, gross jobs. Unless it involved mice or mouse poop, he was willing to do any of the icky stuff (but he left *all* the mousy tasks to his little brother).

"Let's swing past the grocery store on the way back to the campground," Lucy suggested. "Then Dad and I can get started mixing up some dough while you two do the gross jobs."

"Gross jobs!" Herb chanted. "Gross! Gross! Gross! Gross!"

Freddy felt relaxed, happy, and hopeful. The Peach Pie Truck was running smoothly, the past week had been filled with plenty of adventure and fun, the whole family was enjoying doing something together, and—according to Herb's calculations—they were finally making money. *Real* money.

But the best part was, Freddy was starting to discover his true calling: he was *great* at running a business. He couldn't ace a math test, but he excelled at customer service. He knew how to deal with all the weird customers, and his family had begun to rely on him to run the front window. For the first time in his life, Freddy was actually *better* than anyone else—even Lucy—at something.

In a moment of sudden pride and solidarity, Freddy thrust his hand, palm down, into the center of the food truck. "Pile up!" he told the rest of his family. "Peach power!"

Lucy solemnly placed her hand on top of Freddy's. Herb stuffed his own sweaty hand into the stack, and then Dad piled on his hand, too.

"Peach power!" the three kids cried, flinging their hands high.

"Peach power," Dad repeated a second later, wiggling his hands slowly in midair.

"Yeah, that cheer's gonna need some more work," Freddy said with a laugh. "But you know what? It's a start." He winked. "We'll get there."

From the Sketchbook of Freddy Peach:
BEARDS!
- - - - - - - -

In two days at the Madison Blues Music Festival, I witnessed some truly amazing facial hair. Beard labels © Freddy Peach.

The Slug

The Yeti

The Chops

The Walrus

The All-Rounder

The Abe Lincoln

The Turd

The Pencil

The Chin Tuft

The Drowned Rat

The Handlebar

15

EATING PROFITS

Lucy sat in the back corner of the food truck on Monday morning, counting bills from their weekend haul for the twentieth time. She reported the total number to Herb, who did some quick calculations on the back of a napkin.

"We *finally* made a profit," he announced. A huge smile lit up his face, and Lucy leaned forward to give her little brother a hug.

"Music festivals are our scene!" Freddy cheered.

"Yes, indeed!" Dad hollered from the truck's big front sales window. Then he adjusted his hat, popped open the fridge to grab a fresh pie, and made an OK sign with his fingers. "Music festivals are da bomb!"

Freddy groaned. "No, Dad. Just . . . no."

Dad kicked the refrigerator closed and balanced a

pie on his palm. He boomed, "Madison Blues Fest for the win. We be jammin'!"

Lucy snorted a laugh. Herb giggled and raced over to offer his dad a high five. It had been a great weekend—they'd had solid sales, the family had gotten along and cooperated really well, and that morning they'd eaten the yummiest cinnamon buns ever at a farmer's market in downtown Madison.

Feeling light and cheerful, Lucy stuffed all the pie cash into a big zippered envelope and stored it inside the small safe that was bolted into one of the food truck's cabinets. "I'm glad we decided to stay here one extra day," she said. That morning, the Peaches had set up shop on a busy street near the University of Wisconsin–Madison, hoping to sell some fresh-baked slices of pie to college students. They'd had a steady stream of customers from the moment they'd opened. "Madison is obviously our lucky city!"

"Hello," Freddy said to someone outside the window a moment later. "Welcome to the Peach Pie Truck. What can I get for you?"

"I *want* a slice of pie," the woman's friendly voice said. "But what I *need* is a peek at your permit."

Lucy stilled. She scooted a few feet to the left, until she could see the person outside the window. A cop!

Dad dropped the pie he was holding on the counter, and gooey whipped cream splattered everywhere. "Our, ah, *permit*?" he said, obviously flustered. "Yes, of course."

The police officer nodded somberly, then lowered the kickstand on her police bike. "Your pies look quite tasty, but you can't sell here without the right paperwork."

Based on Dad's worried expression, Lucy had a sinking suspicion they didn't *have* the right paperwork. This stop had been unplanned and not part of Dad's original schedule, after all. For a moment, Lucy considered stepping forward to try to charm the officer into letting them go with nothing more than a warning. But she wasn't a fool, and she knew that wasn't going to work. Stuff like that only worked in movies.

As Lucy picked at her thumbnail and tried to figure out how she was going to fix yet another problem, Freddy stepped in front of Dad and said, "You're looking for our permit, Officer? Perhaps I can interest you in a slice of apple crumb pie instead?"

"Apple crumb *is* my favorite." The policewoman gave Freddy a curt smile. "But that's not gonna do the trick. I'm sure you all know there's a hefty fine for selling without a license. If I can just take a peek at your paperwork, we should be able to work this out." Freddy nodded, but Lucy knew even Freddy's sweet-talking wasn't going to make the officer go away without a good, solid look at a permit.

Dad shuffled through the stuff under the counter and pulled out the printed piece of paper that gave them permission to sell pies at the weekend music festival. Lucy sidled up beside her dad, her eyes quickly scanning the paperwork. The permit said nothing about State Street, or *anywhere* else in Madison, for that matter. Nevertheless, Dad passed the paper to the officer, who shook her head. "I'm sorry," she said. "This was only good at the blues festival this weekend. Doesn't work here in town." Then she reached into her fanny pack and pulled out a little machine to type up a ticket.

As the officer tapped away on her machine, Freddy passed the policewoman a massive slab of apple pie. "This is thanks for all you do," he said in a friendly, carefree voice. "If we can't sell it, this yummy pie ought to go to a good cause."

Lucy watched, impressed, as her brother and the police officer shared a smile. Over the past week, she had begun to notice that Freddy had a special way with people. She'd always thought of *herself* as the fixer, but on this trip, Freddy had swept in to solve most of their problems. Something deep inside her chest loosened when she realized she didn't need to manage this one;

Freddy had it covered. She could just sit back and watch while someone else took charge for a change.

"The pie's not a bribe," Freddy told the police officer, holding his hands up like he was under arrest. "I just wanna make that clear."

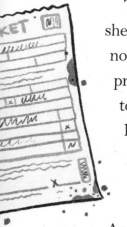

The officer laughed. "Good to know." Then she took a big bite, heaved a contented sigh, and nodded happily. "That's good stuff." Then she printed a ticket and passed it across the counter to Dad. "I really am sorry. I kept the fine as low as I possibly could. But law is law, and if we let people run their food trucks wherever they wanted, well . . . we just can't. Have a nice day now."

As soon as the officer biked away, Lucy took the ticket from her dad's shaking hands. She read it aloud, her eyes widening at the size of the fine. "Guess Madison's not so lucky anymore. This weekend's profits?" she said, closing her eyes. "To pay this ticket, we're about to spend every last penny we just made."

Freddy plucked the ticket out of her hand and hid it behind his back. "It's just a hiccup."

"That's one expensive hiccup," Lucy muttered.

Dad rubbed his forehead and closed his eyes. "What was I thinking?" he groaned quietly. "We're out of our league. I don't know why I thought this was—" he stammered. "If your mother were here—"

Lucy waited for him to say more. To say that it was time to quit. When the going got tough, Walter Peach got going.

"It's a tiny, itty-bitty hiccup," Freddy said again. Lucy spun to face her brother, who was grinning from ear to ear. "Our first ticket. We'll make the money back tomorrow, if we do things right. We just have to learn from this and move on."

"Move on? How?" Lucy whispered, so quietly she wasn't even sure anyone heard her. But then Herb wrapped his spindly little arms around her waist, and she had a feeling she'd said it louder than she'd meant to. She turned to face their dad, to see what he would say.

"Freddy's right. We have to learn from this and move on," Dad said with a resigned shrug. "That's exactly what your mother would want us to do. It's what we need to do."

"No experiment runs smoothly at every stage, right?" Freddy said. "Sometimes stuff fails miserably. But we just gotta move forward and do things differently next time."

"Do things differently . . . ," Dad muttered.

"To Chicago?" Herb asked hopefully.

Freddy glanced over at Lucy. She shrugged. *Why not?* Their experiment was a mess, but maybe Freddy was right: it didn't mean they had to give up and back away. Maybe they could turn this mess into something?

Lucy nodded. "Let's head to Chicago."

Dad didn't say anything; he was blinking like he had something in his eye.

"To Chicago," Freddy agreed.

MADISON MONEY:
(BY HERB)

* Cost of Pie Supplies: $743
* Sales: $1,945!
* Total Profit: $1,202
* Ticket Cost: $1,200
* Total Profit AFTER ticket: $2

Dear Great Aunt Lucinda,

Big news from the Peach Pie Truck: We finally made a profit! But THEN . . . we had to use all that money to pay off a ticket we got for selling pie without a permit in downtown Madison. You know what's crazy, though? Even though things haven't been going perfectly, I'm actually having a pretty good time. Dad even let us stop at a mini-golf course yesterday! I really, really hope we make enough money so Dad will decide that this summer was worth it. I don't think I can go back to the way things were before, not now that I've seen what life is like when our family is kind of a family again. . . .

Miss you and the pups SO MUCH!

Love,
Lucy

HOW TO SPEND A MILLION DOLLARS

When I have a million bucks, I'm going to golf 18 holes at every single PGA golf course, and use the snack cart as my cart so I can get soda and candy whenever I want. With a million bucks, there'd probably be enough money left over to pay all the guys with green Masters jackets to come out and cheer for me.

16

RESTLESS HERB

Herb was hot, sticky, and sad. His dad had promised him that he would get to go swimming *every* day during their trip. But he hadn't even gotten to pop his *toes* in a lake, river, or pool the *whole time* they were in Madison.

The previous day, he'd splashed and waded for a few seconds in a little fountain in the middle of hole thirteen at a mini-golf course. But before he'd even begun to cool off and enjoy himself, Lucy had yelled at him to "GET OUT! THERE ARE PROBABLY DISGUSTING, GERMY THINGS GROWING IN THERE!" (As if he hadn't *checked* first!) So he'd only gotten his sandals and knees wet, which meant it really didn't count as swimming. Then, Lucy had forced him to take a shower and scrub his body extra hard with gross-smelling soap to wash away the fountain water, and showers were icky.

To make matters worse, the campground the Peaches had settled into just outside Chicago had no pool, no sprinklers, no waterslides, no lake, and no stream—which meant Herb was, once again, dry and miserable. This was an outrage. He was trapped inside a stuffy tent every night, squeezed into a stinky food truck every day (but given no tasks or trust at all), and the only thing he truly needed to make him happy—water—was impossible to find. They were in the Midwest, not the desert, and his dad had *promised*. Swimming every day had been Herb's *goal* for their trip, and it was starting to seem like no one was taking his goal seriously. Just like they never took *him* seriously. They made fun of his empty toilet paper roll collection, they'd laughed at his dog-walking business, no one ever wanted to play with his mice, and now *this*.

Lucky Lucy was making progress on *her* goal of finishing every book on the seventh-grade summer reading list. It was sort of annoying how focused she was on her goal, actually. Every time Herb wanted to play cards at the campground, or do the license plate game while they were driving, or play tic-tac-toe on the chalkboard menu outside their pie truck, Lucy said no because she wanted to sneak in a few minutes of reading time. Well, *la-di-da*.

And no one had forgotten about *Freddy's* goal of stopping at weird roadside attractions. They'd even gone out of their way to see that giant, creepy fish!

Dad was also well on his way to succeeding at *his* goal of getting the Peach Pie Truck ready to compete in the Ohio Food Truck Festival—*no one* had forgotten about that part of their experiment. Dad didn't actually seem to care about much of anything, except making sure they were ready to win.

But when it came time to focus on Herb's simple, easy-peasy plan to swim every day? He was starting to get the sense that his goals didn't matter.

Herb was feeling restless, especially after Freddy had told him he couldn't "waste expensive ingredients" making Herb's Cinnaballs anymore. This made Herb grumpy; his cinnaballs were the only way he'd been able to be a part of the family business. No one ever let him try to make real crusts anymore, and he wasn't even allowed to mix up the peach mush for their pies. So now, in the evenings when the other three members of his family were baking and preparing stuff to sell the next day, Herb had nothing to do.

To make matters worse, Herb's pet mice had also begun to outgrow the small, no-fun space inside their little tank. The three mouse babies looked miserable.

Because Herb himself was squished and trapped much of the time, he knew exactly how his little friends felt. It was no fun at all to be stuck inside such cramped quarters every day, with no freedom to roam or choose what they wanted to do.

Herb knew he should probably release his mice when they got a little older—it was the kind and right thing to do, Lucy had told him. Herb understood that. They were born in the wild, so they deserved to return to the wild—they just weren't quite ready to be on their own yet. And to tell the truth, Herb wasn't ready to let them go. They needed him. But still, he wished they could explore a bit of the world outside their tank *now*. How boring, to spend every day inside a glass tank or a cardboard box. They could *see* the rest of the world, but they couldn't get out and explore it. Herb knew what *that* was like.

That's when Herb realized, even if he couldn't control his *own* fate, he could improve life for his mice!

So while the rest of his family worked on baking the pies they would sell in downtown Chicago the next day, Herb got to work on a fun task of his own. First, he filled his arms with a pile of stiff cardboard he found at the campground's recycling station. Then, slowly and quietly, he dragged his supplies into the tent he was now sharing with Lucy. (The four Peaches had begun trading off tent partners each night, since Dad snored— bad. Lucy and Freddy had protested when Herb first brought up the idea of swapping tent-buddies, but after a lot of discussion about it, Lucy had announced that it was only fair that they take turns sleeping next to the snoring machine. Herb felt pretty sure Lucy just wanted a chance to sleep in the same tent as him and his mice and his stuffed pig.)

That evening, no one paid any attention to Herb coming or going out of the family's campsite, which was probably for the best. Herb knew his sister and brother would probably try to take over his project and boss him around if they knew what he was planning (because it was a *good* and *fun* idea), and he wanted to do something nice for his pets all on his own.

The first thing Herb did after he dragged all that cardboard inside the tent was to stuff Lucy's pillow under his own pillow for safekeeping—right next to his stuffed pig. Next, he pushed all the books and sleeping bags to the outside edges of the tent, creating a big open space in the center. Then, he covered the floor of the tent with cardboard. After, he tucked and folded more pieces of cardboard along the edges of the sleeping bags to create four upright walls in the middle of the tent.

As soon as that was done, he placed his entire collection of empty toilet paper rolls into the big open space. They made perfect tunnels and hills for the mice to play in and chew! Herb *knew* his new collection would come in handy for something.

Last, he spread little globs of peanut butter all over the play area, to make it even more enticing. "Voila!" he whispered, admiring his masterpiece. Finally, he plucked each of his mice out of their container and gently lowered them into their very own, Herb-created, cardboard play zone. "Isn't this fun?" he asked the mice, peering over the edge of his homemade mouse run. "Freddy and Lucy built something like this for me in the backyard once."

The mice went wild in their new space. They scrambled through the tunnels, scurried up cardboard ramps, and gobbled up the peanut butter. Best of all, they couldn't escape, because of Herb's cleverly mounted sidewalls. It was like a giant playpen! Herb perched on his knees, peering over the wall of his mouse village. Then, feeling left out, he clambered over the wall and sat inside the pen with his mouse friends.

The smallest, lightest-brown mouse (the one Herb

had named Fuzzy) loved hiding inside the little cardboard tunnels, and often poked his nose out to squeak at his pals as they passed. The medium-brown, chubby mouse (that Herb had named Lump) galloped in great circles around the wide-open space, climbing over Herb's leg and sometimes trying to sneak up inside his pants! And Hound (the biggest, friendliest mouse, who had been named after the sweet dog in the Penderwicks series) seemed to enjoy it when Herb picked him up and placed him in new corners that he could explore. "I'm a mousy tour guide," he said, giggling. Then he sang, "Hound goes here, Hound goes there, Hound goes every-everywhere."

It was nice to see his pets happily exploring their new world. He loved that he could do something for his little pals, that he could help improve their conditions. Herb decided he was starting to become a pretty good caretaker. Forget Herb's Cinnaballs—he could spend his nights making mouse exploration areas!

Suddenly, a loud *ziiiiip!* shook Herb out of his reverie. The tent flap flew open and Lucy poked her nose inside their newly redesigned tent space. *"Herb!"* his sister screeched, after she'd had time to get a good look at his creation.

"Yes?" Herb replied sweetly. He cringed; Lucy looked grouchy. Perhaps she'd been stuck in the kitchen too long. He lifted Hound and held the big mouse up in front of Lucy's face. "Want to hold him? He likes it when you rub between his ears."

His sister glared at him. "If I find *one* mouse poop in my bed tonight, you will pay," she growled.

"I'll clean everything up. I promise." Herb said.

Lucy knew he would. Herb *never* broke promises. She nodded, satisfied. With a final huff, she dug her toothbrush and face wash out of her bag and zipped the tent flap closed again.

"Do we have time to read a chapter of our book before bed?" Herb called after her. Lucy didn't respond, but he was pretty sure her loud grunt and angry footsteps meant *N-O* no.

THE MIDWEST

17

CHICAGO CHARACTERS

Freddy had always known he didn't have the same type of smarts as the other members of his family. Lucy, Herb, and Dad had all mastered math facts, none of them ever got distracted during tests or projects, and everyone except Freddy had done brainy stuff that won prizes. Freddy never won prizes and, no matter how much he practiced, he was certain he would never remember how to multiply fractions.

Perhaps this was because Freddy's head was filled to bursting with random facts, strange world records, art project ideas, and a few rather unimpressive card tricks. None of the things that occupied his brain ever earned him a perfect score on standardized tests, but he continually held out hope that someday his type of smarts and knowledge would prove useful for *something*.

Though he had read about a lot of amazing things over the past few years (fun facts about pee, an island that was home to a colony of swimming pigs, hundreds of scary-but-true survival stories), Freddy rarely experienced anything truly exciting in real life. His classmates were all very nice, but also fairly ordinary; his hometown was safe and pretty, nestled on the shore of majestic Lake Superior, but it was also pretty boring. If he was lucky, he crossed paths with one or two particularly interesting people on any given day—while he was at the library, selecting apples at the grocery store, or waiting to be picked up after his swimming lessons at the Y.

Which was why it was so exciting that, on the Peach family's first day of business in downtown Chicago, Freddy met more interesting people than he would usually encounter in a whole *year* at home. During the course of the day, he gave all their customers nicknames and jotted them down in his sketchbook. He knew this would help him remember them all, so he could draw pictures of some of them later.

"Could I please try a sample of your apple pie?" A hulking, muscled guy wearing a SMILE tank top flashed Freddy a friendly smile just a few minutes after the Peach Pie Truck had opened. The man's hair was shaved around the edges, but the top was long and pushed back with gel or sweat or *something*.

"Sorry," Freddy told the guy. "We don't offer samples."

"I just . . . ," the man began. "Never mind. It's not your problem." Then the big guy began to cry. Loud, blubbering sobs that echoed off the buildings around them.

Freddy and Lucy exchanged a nervous look. Herb gaped at the man, while Dad pretended to be busy washing something in the sink. Meanwhile, the guy pulled napkin after napkin out of their dispenser, loudly snorting and wiping his nose.

Dad, clearly uncomfortable, stepped forward and looked beseechingly at Freddy. He mouthed, "What should we do?"

Unfazed, Freddy quickly said, "Which pie was it you were hoping to taste, sir?"

The guy blinked. He blubbered, "I—I'd love a quick sample of the apple." He gobbled it down, and then belched and said, "That's yummy. Now the peach?"

Freddy sliced a slim sliver off the peach pie and passed it to the man.

"Mmm-mmm," the man said. "I'd just love to compare that to the French silk." He ate that, and then said, "Seems a shame not to test the pecan and turtle, too. That's the only way I can make an informed decision. And if I don't try them all, one of the pies will feel left out."

Lucy narrowed her eyes at the guy. Freddy squeezed his sister's shoulder to try to calm her. In the grand scheme of things, a few free slivers of pie really weren't a big deal.

"All scrumptious," the man—whom Freddy had now secretly nicknamed Sample Stan—announced, after swallowing down his sliver of turtle pie. "Sadly, I couldn't eat another bite."

Then Sample Stan turned and strolled away. Freddy knew they'd been had. But when Dad congratulated him on how well he'd handled the situation, saying he'd demonstrated grace, kindness, compassion, and smart thinking, he decided he really didn't care. He'd much rather make his dad proud than sell a sneaky dude a slice of five-dollar pie. It felt good to do something well, and have Dad take notice.

After Sample Stan stopped by, they met:

- Quick and Crabby
- Big Guy Flirts with Dad
- Pays in Coins (five bucks' worth of nickels and dimes!)
- Toddlers Who Touch Stuff
- Overly Curious Customer

- Job Seeker ("Are you guys hiring? Can I get an application?")
- Discount Lady ("I'll give you three dollars for a slice. Five seems high.")
- Bathroom Hunter
- Tattoos + an Iguana (an ACTUAL, LIVE IGUANA on the dude's arm!)
- Nearly Naked
- Sings His Order ("I will take peeeeeeach piiiiiiiie!")
- Dine & Dash
- Burpie McBurperson
- Hold the Crust
- Side of Fries
- Barter Boy
- Cast of Hamilton (two REAL actors from the Chicago cast ensemble!!)

Late in the afternoon, a soft-spoken lady with a real, live *parrot* on her shoulder strolled up to the truck. "Do you have cake?" she asked Freddy, carefully studying the five-item menu. She looked nervous, her eyes flicking quickly between Freddy, the menu, her parrot, and something invisible on the sidewalk over her left shoulder.

"Nope," Freddy replied. "Just the five pies, clearly listed there on the board. Is that a parrot?"

"Chocolate cake?" the woman asked, ignoring his question.

"We have no cake at all." He squinted. "Does it just sit there? Does it ever try to fly away?"

"Red velvet?" Cake Lady asked, stroking one of the parrot's spindly claws.

Freddy shook his head, keeping careful watch on the bird. "We're the Peach *Pie* Truck, ma'am. No red velvet."

"You know what's yummy? Vanilla cake with raspberry filling and buttercream frosting."

"Good to know." Freddy smiled at her patiently. "Can I tempt you with a slice of pie today? The French silk is very popular. It's cake-*like*, I guess."

Cake Lady pulled her eyebrows together. "That will be fine." She slid a fiver across the counter and collected her pie. "And I'll come by tomorrow to see if cake is back in stock."

Surrounded by all these odd and fascinating folks roaming the streets of Chicago, Freddy began to wonder who would win the prize for Strangest Food Truck Customer Ever. The only thing he knew for sure was, Chicago had presented plenty of challenges that gave the Peaches a perfect chance to practice their customer service skills for the Ohio Food Truck Festival.

STRANGEST
FOOD TRUCK
CUSTOMER

During the course of their trip, Freddy had begun to realize he had a knack for dealing with people. And he felt even *more* confident about his people skills after handling all of Chicago's kooky customers. If they managed to come out on top at the Ohio Food Truck Festival, Freddy knew it would be in big part because of contributions *he'd* made to this family experiment. Sure, they were a team—and everyone in the family played an important role. But for once in his life, Freddy felt a little like the leader. He, Freddy Peach, was *good* at this. And he couldn't wait to help guide his family to victory.

CHICAGO MONEY:
(BY HERB)

* Cost of Pie Supplies: $532
  (Dad didn't ruin any pies!)
* Sales: $1,250 *
* Returns: $5
  (Cake Lady didn't like her pie)
* Total Profit: $713!!!!! **

* Thanks to Freddy, who convinced the campground manager to let us sell some of our leftover pie to other campers!
**Not $10,000 yet, but it's a step in the right direction . . . and we still have time!

18

LATE-NIGHT REVELATIONS

The Peaches set off out of Chicago early Friday afternoon, hoping to beat rush-hour traffic. But it turned out rush hour lasted for *many* hours in Chicago, and their giant beast of a truck was jammed between semitrucks, honking cars, and angry minivans, all trying to elbow their way out of the city. They finally made it across the bridge between Illinois and Indiana just as the sun tucked itself into the horizon. It was that magical hour when the sky was awash in pink and orange, and even the concrete jungle outside the food truck's dusty front window looked beautiful, streaked with gentle color.

Dad was hoping to make it as far as Ann Arbor, Michigan, that night, but Lucy had a feeling they would have to stop somewhere to sleep along the way. Everyone was wiped out. As had become tradition, Lucy sat beside Dad in the front seat of the truck, quietly reading her book while he listened to podcasts and dictated research notes and reminders to himself on his cell phone. Freddy and Herb had both conked out as soon as they were clear of stop-and-go traffic, so Lucy and Dad were left alone in peace and quiet up front.

While they drove through the congested suburban roadways outside Chicago, Lucy marveled at her newfound realization: she was actually enjoying their trip, at least a little bit. It was nice to see her family united by a goal, even if the goal did involve a lot of hard work. And because they were doing this whole thing in Mom's honor, Lucy actually wanted to help the Great Peach Experiment succeed. She'd seen her dad get passionate about work projects plenty of times before, of course, but none of those ventures had ever involved or interested her; they'd just been excuses for him to disappear. With the Peach Pie Truck, however, everything felt different. Lucy was starting to sense that things were changing; she had begun to feel like life was creeping a little closer to the way it used to be.

"Dad?" Lucy said, yawning as they passed Gary, Indiana. She was hungry and sleepy and the book she was reading had not yet captured her attention. On both sides of the highway, lines of smokestacks belched steam into the air, offering a stark contrast to Chicago's bright and shiny skyline. "You said you used to take road trips with your cousins when you were a kid?"

Dad nodded. "Yep."

"With Great Aunt Lucinda, right?" Lucy asked.

"Indeed," Dad said quietly.

"Will you tell me about some of those trips?" Lucy asked, settling deeper into her seat. She knew very little about Dad's childhood, only that his mom had died when he was still in elementary school. And Lucy's grandpop had been in the army, so they had moved around a lot when Dad was growing up. He didn't talk about it much, but Lucy got the feeling that Dad and Grandpop had never been very close. Though he died before Herb was born and they hadn't visited him very often when he was still alive, Lucy could remember the smell of his cigars, and the way he laughed out loud when he rubbed his prickly beard stubble on her cheek.

"Sure," Dad said. He changed the channel to a pop music station. Then he told Lucy how, every summer starting when he was eight, Dad had joined Aunt Lucinda, Uncle Martin, and his cousins on their road trips. "Some of my happiest memories are from those adventures," he said. "We'd stop and camp at night, cooking dinner over the fire. My cousins and I would poke around in the woods and explore fun little towns during the day. One summer, we drove up to a water park in Canada. Another time, we stopped to explore some caves in Kentucky. But the best trips came later—when Lucinda and Martin drove us all the way across the country to North Carolina, right on the Atlantic Ocean, and we camped close to the beach for a week." Dad gazed out the windshield into the hazy night sky. "We'd swim, play in the waves, eat ice cream for lunch. I liked swimming back then just as much as Herb does now."

"Why haven't we ever done that?" Lucy asked, feeling bold for just coming out and saying something that was on her mind. She'd blurted out questions to her mom, plenty of times, but it was harder with Dad.

"Everything's different now," he said wistfully. "Prices out East have shot up, the campgrounds have all been bought out to build big houses and hotels, and hurricanes keep eroding the beaches. Also, with work as busy as it is, it's just an awfully long way to go to sit around and do nothing."

Lucy frowned. "Why was it Aunt Lucinda and Uncle Martin who took you? Why didn't Grandpop go along?"

"My father didn't get much time off work, so trips like that never made sense," Dad said. "That's just the way it was." There was silence for a few moments while neither of them said anything more.

Lucy considered the way things used to be in her family and wondered if Dad ever thought about how much things had changed since Mom died. She felt a little guilty for thinking it, but everything had been so much better before. Lucy often wondered if their life would ever go completely back to normal.

Finally, Dad flipped on a podcast, explaining, "I'm starting to get sleepy—do you mind if I turn this on so I have something to focus on? Still hoping to make it to Ann Arbor tonight so we don't lose a day of sales tomorrow. We're really in the zone, and I don't want to lose momentum in the weeks leading up to the Food Truck Festival. Lots to do to if we want to be ready for the big event so we can call this summer a success."

"Go ahead," Lucy said. She opened her book and pretended to read. But the words just swam in front of her eyes. She was too busy trying to process what her dad had said. The beach didn't sound like *nothing* to her. All of the trips Dad had taken with his cousins and Great Aunt Lucinda sounded marvelous. Obviously, they *had* been wonderful, or he wouldn't have such fond memories.

A summer of blissful nothing, without a care in the world. Could the four of them ever have an adventure like that? She tried to imagine what it would be like to spend time together as a family, doing something—or nothing—with the only goal being to enjoy one another's company. They used to do that all the time when Mom was still around. But no matter how hard Lucy wished she could get that old life back, her wish didn't seem likely to come true.

This trip wasn't quite like the ones Dad and his cousins used to take, but it *was* a chance for the Peaches to create a few special new memories as a family. If the Great Peach Experiment could help patch up some of the holes in their lives, Lucy decided it would be worth giving up half her summer break to bake and sell pies. Figuring out some way to paint her dad back into the picture would be a game changer.

They were bumping along I-94, making surprisingly good time, when suddenly the food truck began to hiss. It whined, clanked, and then steam began to puff out of the slits on either side of the hood. Lucy glanced at her dad, who didn't appear to have noticed *any* of these things. He was lost in another world. "Dad?"

"Eh?" Dad said softly.

"The truck is smoking."

"Goodness me!" Dad shrieked. "The truck *is* smoking."

Freddy and Herb both stirred in the back seat,

craning their necks to look out the windshield as the truck lurched and swayed briefly out of its lane. There was a sign announcing the exit for a town called Jackson, Michigan. Lucy glanced at the atlas and discovered that Jackson was the largest town around for miles. Hopefully they could find a mechanic—and if not, at least a small town was better than being broken down on the side of the road. "Exit here," Lucy told him. "I think we're going to need help."

From the Sketchbook of Freddy Peach:
HOW TO SPEND A MILLION DOLLARS

When I'm rich, I'm going to fly to space . . . or at the very least, fly SOMEWHERE cool, like an undiscovered planet that looks like the giant bean sculpture in downtown Chicago. (I know the Bean is right there in the middle of downtown, so it's not technically a RANDOM roadside attraction—but it was still very cool.)

19

HAPPY CAMPGROUND

Herb had decided that this campground—the one they checked into after their truck broke down—was his new favorite place.

First, there was a pool. A real, honest-to-goodness *pool* with warm water, a deepish section, ladders, a comfy reading chair for Lucy, and water noodles they could use for battles and water horse races.

Second, there was *also* a lake—one you could swim in, with canoes anyone was allowed to borrow, and a sauna that magically stayed warm all day long!

Third, there was a game room with two video game machines (PAC-MAN and a deer-hunting game), a pool table, and even *more* comfy chairs.

Fourth, and most important, the check-in guy sold soft-serve ice cream right at the front desk!

But the cherry on top of it all was, the campground offered a seven-dollar all-you-can-eat buffet breakfast where Herb was allowed to get Frosted Flakes, a bagel (which he wrapped up in a napkin for later), *and* make his very own cinnamon waffle in a special waffle machine.

Herb had dubbed it Happy Campground. *This* was the good life. *Better* than a hotel, even.

The previous night, after Dad had pulled the truck off the highway and rumbled into a service station, Herb had perused lottery tickets (which his dad *still* refused to buy, even though Herb reminded him to "just think about it" every time they stopped) while he listened to Dad and Lucy talking to the man in charge. He'd overheard the man say that all the mechanic shops were closed until morning, but they were welcome to leave the truck there for the night until someone could come and take a look at it.

So, all four Peaches (along with one tank of mice, two tents, and three big bags of gear) loaded into the gas station attendant's minivan, left their weary food truck behind, and got a ride to the nearest campground. It was late—almost ten o'clock—when they checked in, but Lucy begged Dad to let Herb take a quick swim before bed to get the wiggles out. As he settled into his sleeping bag, wet hair soaking into his pillow and stuffed pig, Herb felt pretty sure he had never gone to sleep happier.

First thing the next morning, Dad headed back to the service station to check on the food truck, while Herb and his siblings enjoyed a whole morning *free*! No baking, no cleaning, no planning, no strange customers, no generator humming, no pie smell in the air, *nothing*.

Glorious, glorious nothing.

It was perfect.

Herb spent part of the morning collecting empty toilet paper rolls for his mice to chew on and play with. Next, he found a few choice pine cones that he added to the box he'd been filling with nature souvenirs from their trip. Then he and his siblings swam until their fingers and toes were wrinkled and pruney, played a

few games of pool, and ate watermelon left over from the breakfast buffet. After, they each got an ice cream cone and roamed around the campground, checking out other campsites while Freddy introduced himself to their neighbors.

After they'd been wandering for a bit, Freddy tossed more than half his ice cream into a big dumpster. "I can't eat this," he groaned. "I can't believe I'm about to say this, but I'm officially sweeted out. I've eaten too much pie these past two weeks. If I eat any more, I'm gonna need to pull a Herb." Then, to make sure the other two understood what he was saying, he pantomimed puking. "Did you know that the pumpkin pie–eating champion earned a world record after she ate fifty pieces of pump- kin pie in ten minutes?"

"Gross," Herb said. "I dare you to try to beat that."

Freddy filled his cheeks with air, then blew it out again—making a glurching, vomity noise. "I pass."

"I know I'm not supposed to say this, but is anyone else kinda glad our truck broke?" Herb asked softly, glancing at his siblings.

"Yes," Freddy and Lucy said in unison. Herb kicked a stone, watching it roll down one of the dirt-crusted lanes that crisscrossed the campground.

"The past couple weeks have actually been pretty fun," Lucy admitted, as Herb slipped his small hand inside her bigger one. "Exploring Minneapolis was great. And I liked selling pies to all those bearded dudes at the music festival in Madison, even though we got that ticket. Chicago was cool, too. But I'm not sure I can survive another two weeks of baking and working in the food truck. . . ." Herb caught his sister glancing at Freddy. "I know it's really important to you and Dad that we make some real money and win the Ohio Food Truck Festival, Freddy, but—"

Herb cut her off. "But hard work is hard?"

Lucy laughed. "Exactly. And if it were *just* the Food Truck Festival we had left, that would be one thing. But another few weeks running the Peach Pie Truck might actually kill me! Don't you guys ever just want to do *nothing*?"

"We can't give up now," Freddy said seriously. Then he shook his head and plucked a perfect stick out of the wooded area at the edge of the campground. Just as Herb was jealously admiring his brother's glorious find, Freddy broke the stick in half and handed Herb the longer piece, so they could have a stick battle. "But yeah, I hear you—a break *would* be nice. I'd love to have a little more time to draw and explore and stuff."

Herb slapped his stick against his brother's. "I forgot. How do they decide the winner of the Food Truck Festival, Freddy?" Maybe, Herb thought, they could just take the next few weeks off to swim and play and relax here at Happy Campground, and then they could head straight to Delaware, Ohio, for Dad's big competition.

"People vote for their favorite truck, based on taste and customer service," Freddy explained. "Then they combine customer votes with how much money each truck earns during the Festival, and that's how they figure out each truck's total score."

"So basically, we're a shoo-in," Lucy giggled. "We've made . . . how much so far? Negative dollars on this trip?"

"We're not exactly running like a well-oiled machine," Freddy muttered, kicking his stick high with the toe of his sneaker.

Herb swung his and Lucy's linked hands through the air. "Well, hopefully they have some oil for the truck at the service station. Then we'll be well-oiled, right?"

"Oh, Herbie," Lucy said, laughing. "If only it were that simple."

Dear Great Aunt Lucinda,

Dad told me about some of the road trips he used to take with you and Uncle Martin. They must have been so much fun! I hope someday our family can have adventures like that. Without Mom, we haven't really had much fun as a family the past couple years— but I think things are finally getting better? This Experiment is helping us figure out how to work together, at least a little bit. But what happens if we fail? We CAN'T fail. We just can't.

Miss you!

Lucy

20

DAD'S PLAN

Freddy had just finished eating a monster-sized break-fast at the campground's buffet on Sunday morning when Dad traipsed into the dining area with a big smile on his face.

"*Really* good news," Dad said.

All the kids looked up hopefully. "We're staying here in Michigan?" Herb asked.

"They canceled the art fair in Columbus?" Freddy guessed. Because of their truck's mechanical trouble, they had been forced to skip their next planned stop in Ann Arbor, Michigan, and were heading straight down to Ohio instead. Dad had paid for a permit to sell pie at some kind of art fair in the city of Columbus. Freddy wiggled his eyebrows, and said, "So you're thinking we should stop in Sandusky and go on roller coasters at

Cedar Point instead? Did you know that's the Roller Coaster Capital of the World?"

Dad gave him a strange look. "A different kind of good news," he clarified. "They have a Laundromat right here on-site at the campground!"

"*That's* the really good news?" Lucy asked.

"We can finally catch up on some of the important stuff that's fallen by the wayside while we've been dealing with other things," Dad explained.

"And the 'important stuff' in this equation is laundry?" Lucy guessed.

Dad went on, "That's right. Lucy. I'd like you to gather up all our dirty rags, clothes, and blankets and spend the day handling laundry duty."

"Why do *I* have to go to the creepy Laundromat?" Lucy huffed.

"We all need to do our piece," Dad barked. "You've got to step up and do your fair share or this whole experiment will fall apart."

Freddy watched his sister's eyes widen. What did Dad think Lucy had been doing this whole *trip*? And what did he think she'd been doing for the past two *years*? Lucy always did her fair share. *More* than her fair share.

After their mom died, Lucy had been the one to

comfort Freddy and Herb during the scary months that followed. She helped them get breakfast every morning, she took them to the park and built forts and read them stories when their dad was working, she created fun scavenger hunts for them when Dad brought them along to his science conventions, and she had even taught Freddy how to make French toast and scrambled eggs all by himself, so he didn't always need to rely on her to feed him. In many ways, the past few years had been one big, fat experiment (and not the fun kind). But Lucy always—*always*—stepped up to do her part and more.

"That's not fair," Freddy blurted out after a split-second's hesitation. "Lucy shouldn't be the only one stuck doing laundry."

"I can do it," Herb offered.

"You're too little," Dad told him.

Herb squeezed his lips into a thin line. "I could try."

Freddy had witnessed his little brother trying— over and over throughout this trip—to contribute and help out in his own special way: by creating Herb's Cinnaballs; by caring for and entertaining his (terrifying) mice; by keeping tally of their truck profits with his Tiny Genius math skills; by offering Lucy hugs, even when their sister wouldn't admit she needed one. But mostly, Herb never gave up hope that their broken family was capable of succeeding at something together, despite all their failures of the past.

Sometimes Herb wasn't much help. But sometimes no one would even give him a chance to try. "Herb can help," Freddy insisted. "We all can. But, Dad, couldn't we wait and do some of this stuff tomorrow? The truck is still getting fixed, and there's a ton of other—funner—things we could do today instead. It *is* Sunday. Don't we deserve a day off?"

"There's the lake, and the pool," Herb chimed in. "I can show you some of my best cannonball moves, and Dad, if you came swimming with us, we'd have even teams for noodle wars." Herb squirmed and bounced on his toes. "Ooh! And the front desk guy told me there's an island in the middle of the lake where you can canoe out and have a picnic! A picnic in the middle of water!"

Even as Herb's excitement built to a crescendo, Dad continued to shake his head. "We just don't have time to waste on nonsense. We've got permits lined up in our next few cities, and there's so much to do to make sure we're ready for the Food Truck Festival. We can use this forced downtime to prepare for the grand finale." He took a deep breath, still shaking his head, and then headed off toward the campground office lobby with his laptop. "Eyes on the prize," he declared, almost entirely to himself. "We've gotta keep our eyes on the prize."

Freddy huffed. He *did* have eyes on the prize; he *desperately* wanted to see this experiment succeed, and to help his family win the Food Truck Festival. He'd *love* to win that cash prize. Being crowned festival champ would be a tangible, obvious mark of success. Even better than a perfect quiz in math. And if Mom were there, Freddy had no doubt they would win. If they failed, Dad would realize none of this had been worth it. Freddy *needed* to make sure they succeeded—for Mom, and for the future of their family.

But even as he considered this, he couldn't help wondering: Was winning the Food Truck Festival really the ultimate prize on this summer trip? Or had they been so focused on their final destination that they'd missed an important turn somewhere along the way?

21

HERB'S DECISION

"I decided it's time," Herb announced to Lucy on Monday morning, right after their dad had set off to collect the fixed-up food truck. Before he left, he had told the kids they had an hour or so left to relax, but that they should be ready to hit the road and get back to work just as soon as he got back from the shop.

"Time for what?" Lucy asked without looking up from her book. She'd been reading in the campground's game room while Herb pretended to play video games. He didn't actually have any quarters to put in the machines, but that didn't matter. It was fun to pretend.

"I've decided to leave my mice here in Michigan," Herb said.

"What?" Lucy glanced up. "Why?"

"They're old enough to take care of themselves now,"

he explained, his bottom lip quivering the slightest bit. "I helped take care of them when they were little, when they needed me most. But they're bigger now and I don't want them to be sad. I love it here, and I know they do, too. I wish *we* could stay here forever, but we can't because we have to go to Ohio. But I *can* leave my mice in the big, grassy field over by the lake, and I think that will make them happy."

Lucy smiled sadly. "Oh, Herbie. That's really sweet of you. I think they'd really like to stay here."

Herb let his sister pull him in for a tight squeeze. Lucy's hugs felt good. And even though they didn't make his sadness go away, they made it shrink just a little bit. "Will you come with me when it's time to say goodbye?" Herb asked.

"Of course I will," Lucy told him. "And I think Freddy will be happy to say goodbye to them, too."

Herb laughed. "Yeah, I think you're right."

🐭 🐭 🐭

A few minutes before Dad was due back at Happy Campground, Herb loaded his mice into a small box. He tucked his favorite T-shirt inside the little enclosure, and Lump nestled right into it. Herb had already decided that he would hide the shirt and box deep behind the woodpile near the campground's sauna, just in case his mice missed him and needed a soft, safe place to sleep at night.

"You've done a really good job of caring for your little friends over the past few weeks, Herb," Lucy told him as she watched Herb get everything ready.

Herb nodded. "I know." He sat on the picnic table with the box cradled in his arms. "Hey, Lucy?"

His sister sat down beside him. "What's up?"

"Sometimes I used to worry that I did something wrong when Mom was sick," he admitted.

Lucy shook her head and pulled him close. "Oh, pal," she whispered. "You didn't."

"I know that," Herb said. "But I used to wonder, if I did a better job taking care of her, maybe I could have saved her?" Lucy took a deep breath and started to say something, but Herb cut her off. "Now that I'm older, I'm pretty sure I did exactly what she needed me to do. I loved her, and I brought her snacks and water when she needed them, and I snuggled close and tried to make her laugh."

"Yeah," Lucy said, her voice shaky. "You did all of that stuff really well."

"I did the same thing for my mice," Herb said, gazing up into his sister's beautiful, kind face. "And now it's time to let them go—just like we had to do with Mom. That's what's best. My mice will be happy to be free; just like Mom needed to be free of her cancer. I know it hurt her a lot at the end."

Lucy nodded, her eyes full of tears. "You're really something, Herb Peach."

"You are, too, Lucy-lu." Herb smiled at her and gazed down at his mice. It was time.

With his siblings in tow, Herb carried his mice through the campground, along the path to the lake. As they trekked across the waterfront, Herb held the box tight and Lucy wrapped her arm around his shoulder. Herb looked up at his sister, and said quietly, "I miss Mom."

Lucy nodded. "Me, too, buddy. Me, too."

Herb paused for a second. "But we're gonna be okay, I think."

Freddy kicked at the grass a few paces off, but Herb knew he was listening.

Lucy sighed, though she didn't say anything.

"We're gonna be okay," Herb repeated. He nodded; he needed his brother and sister to believe it, too. "Things are different now, but different doesn't have to be bad. At least, not all the time. She's not here, but that doesn't mean she's gone."

Herb set off at a slow walk again, stopping when they reached the sauna. There was a big, grassy field stretching out behind the old wooden building, and lots of comfy trees and brushy areas where his mice could set up camp. There were also lots of holes under the building, where his friends could hide out from any bad guys.

"I'm going to miss you," Herb whispered softly to his mice. He held the box close against his chest, hoping his friends could hear and feel the thumping of his heart. "But I'll always remember you." He was pretty sure they understood.

"Fare thee well," Freddy said, saluting formally from afar.

"We'll miss you," Lucy told the mice, placing her hand gently on Herb's shoulder. "Enjoy your new adventures."

Slowly, carefully, Herb lowered the box to the ground. His mice were restless, as if they could sense what was in store for them. One by one, Herb lifted his friends out of the box and set them in the grass. "I love you, Fuzzy," he told the littlest mouse. Fuzzy scrambled out of Herb's hand and sniffed at the air. "I love you, Lump," he told the chubby mouse. Lump lumbered off, immediately hiding under the nearby woodpile. When Herb opened his hand to let Hound out, Hound held back. "Go on, Hound," Herb urged. "I love you, pal. And you're going to love it here. It's way better than the stuffy, hot food truck."

Hound tumbled out of Herb's hand but didn't stray far. Herb so badly wanted to pick his little buddy back up, hide him in his pocket, and keep him forever. But that wasn't what was best for his mouse friend. He'd begun to realize that no matter how tight he held on, sometimes the things he loved needed to be let go.

It was hard to say goodbye, but he was ready.

Herb pushed the box and T-shirt behind the wood-pile, way back where no one would see them. The three mice sniffed at it, and then, together, they set off into their big, new world.

THE MIDWEST

MIDDLE OF MICHIGAN MONEY:
(BY HERB)

* Cost of Pie Supplies, to get ready for the art fair in Ohio: $467
* Sales: $0
* Total Profit: -$467

22

KEEP ON TRUCKIN'

Lucy wasn't quite sure when the mutiny started. But she had noticed a major shift in her siblings' attitudes as soon as they left Michigan.

After Herb bid farewell to his mice, he was quiet for the rest of the day. Her sweet baby brother didn't even want to read a chapter of *The Penderwicks* that night before bed. He just crawled under his covers and closed his eyes. When Lucy crouched over his sleeping bag to kiss his forehead, he didn't roar or make funny faces or attempt a tickle surprise attack like he usually did. He just lay there quietly, pretending he was already asleep. She knew letting the mice go had been hard for him. He didn't like to let *anything* go. She was surprised to realize how much Herb had grown up in the past few years, and even more so in the past few weeks.

Freddy was grumpy, too. As they'd pulled out of Jackson, Michigan, heading southeast toward Columbus, Ohio, Freddy had reminded their dad—for the fourth time—that the World's Largest Cherry Pie Pan (as well as the *second* largest cherry pie pan) was not far away in northern Michigan, and that those were two of the strange roadside attractions he'd been most looking forward to seeing along the way. In response, Dad had said, "Oh, Freddy, stop being silly. We just don't have that kind of time. We can't get sidetracked now, or this whole thing is going to crumble to pieces."

"But," Freddy said, pleading, "you said we could stop and see weird stuff on the trip. That was supposed to be part of the fun—and it's my *goal.* A giant pie pan is too cool and too perfect to miss. We're already *in* Michigan; it can't be that far out of the way!"

Dad snapped, "End of discussion. We need to buckle down and focus on what matters. There's been enough dillydallying."

In Lucy's estimation, there had been almost *no* dillydallying, but who was she to judge? (If Dad had asked Lucy, she would have told him that *he* was the only one who'd done any *real* dillydallying, because he kept sneaking away from the food truck to check in with work. But he didn't ask.)

Then, on Tuesday morning, while they were finishing up all the pies they were hoping to sell at that day's art fair, Lucy discovered they were out of whipped cream for the French silk and turtle pies. "Oh, well," Freddy replied, shrugging one shoulder.

"Oh, well?" Lucy asked, rattled by her brother's bad-itude.

"We'll just get more tomorrow," Freddy grumbled, hastily crossing French silk and turtle pie off their chalkboard menu.

Lucy stared at him in disbelief. From day one, Freddy had been the Peach most committed to this venture. He had flung himself into this crazy idea feet-first, just like their mom would have done. Freddy was constantly brainstorming new pies to try, doing research by chatting with other food truck owners, figuring out clever new ways of drawing customers to the truck, and checking supply levels to make sure they never ran out of any key ingredients. But now, Freddy didn't even seem to care that they were going to lose sales. They were still thousands of dollars away from reaching their goal, yet her brother seemed to have lost some of the Freddy "spark" that had gotten everyone fired up at the beginning of the trip.

As a result, their first day at the art fair was utterly

miserable. And by the second day, somehow each Peach was even *more* lackluster than the day before. When their first customer ordered a slice of apple crumb pie, Freddy unenthusiastically plopped a thick slab of the pie onto her plate and took the customer's money without his usual bright smile. Moments after ambling away, the woman returned to the counter with a disgusted look on her face. "This is terrible!" she said, tossing the pie onto the service counter. *"Awful!"* the woman repeated. "Taste it."

Freddy shook his head. He held up his hands and said, "I'm pied out. I refuse."

So Lucy cut a bite-sized chunk out of the apple pie and popped it in her mouth. She spit it right back out. "Ew! Salt!" she wailed. Someone had obviously used *salt* instead of *sugar* in the apple pie filling, and it tasted absolutely horrible. Lucy secretly wondered if the salt topping had been an accident, or if—maybe—the ingredient switcheroo had been some form of sabotage by one of her brothers.

By the third day of the art fair, business had slowed to a trickle. It was nearing one hundred degrees outside (which meant it was hotter inside the food truck, and even the fridge was struggling to keep cool), so the Peaches closed up shop early and returned to the campground. The four of them settled in around the picnic table at their campsite, sweating and mushy and miserable.

"So tomorrow it's on to Indianapolis," Dad said, scanning Herb's map. Herb had taken the map out of his mouse house after he'd freed his pals at Happy Campground.

Dad's finger traced their path across the map. "We're all set to sell pies at the Indianapolis Motor Show, then we'll head back this way for our grand finale: the big Food Truck Festival in Delaware, Ohio."

"Wait a sec," Lucy said, looking at the map over her dad's shoulder. She pointed and drew a line across the page with her finger. "We're going from Columbus to Indianapolis and then basically *back* to just outside Columbus again? Isn't that a little weird?"

"That's how the permits and schedule worked out," Dad snapped, apparently unconcerned about the fact that they were about to spend five hot, extra hours driving in their enormous truck. "The schedule got a little messed up with our extra days in Michigan, and besides, it's not that far out of the way."

Dad pulled off his hat, revealing a bright red mark encircling his forehead. "I've got to warn you," he said with a deep sigh. "It's going to be a hot couple of days in

Indy. I checked the forecast this morning, and it looks like it's going to be at least ninety-five, with eighty percent humidity."

Lucy could see that Herb was trying to hold back tears. Her brother had never done well in heat when he didn't have some sort of water to cool off in, and the poor kid was bored stiff. He had no one to play with, now that his mice had moved on to greener pastures, and he never got to help with any of the baking. He spent his days playing with a LEGO set (building the same three things over and over again) or drawing with chalk outside the food truck. He'd also started working his way through Freddy's math workbooks for fun.

There was more than a week to go before the Ohio Food Truck Festival started, and Lucy wasn't sure any one of them would make it that long.

"So, tonight," Dad said in a weary voice, "we have a *lot* to do. Herb, you'll come to the store with me so you can cool off in the freezer aisle while we get some more supplies. Lucy, you can start making crusts for the motor show. Freddy, I need you to clean out the truck, and then—"

"What about swimming?" Herb asked, interrupting. "I didn't get to go in the water at all yesterday, and—"

Dad cut him off before he could finish. It was almost as if he hadn't heard Herb at all. Like he'd zoned out and disappeared—just the way he had, over and over again, after Mom died. "Lucy, I'm also going to need you to take another couple loads to the Laundromat, and then if you could get dinner started while—"

"No," Lucy said. The heat had obviously melted the last remnants of her patience, and she suddenly felt something inside her snap. "I'm not doing any of that. It's hot, I'm tired, Herb wants to go swimming, and there's no reason we need to do any of these chores right this second. What's the rush?"

"Lucy," Dad said, his voice equally snappy, "must I remind you that this is a *family* experiment? The whole point of this summer was for us to build something new together, and work hard to succeed." He huffed out a breath and ran a shaking, sweaty hand through his hair. "I refuse to fail at the Food Truck Festival. Failing isn't an option. And as I've told you kids time and again, we can't succeed if we're not all doing our part." He slapped his hat on the table. "If you don't like the way something's working, Lucy, perhaps it's worth taking a closer look at your approach to the process. You can propose a solution and we'll analyze it, then—"

"No!" Lucy growled. "This is *your* experiment, *your* adventure, and you're the parent so it's *your* job to fix it if something's not working. I can't do everything. You want to pretend that this food truck is going to fix us and make everything go back to the way it used to be? Well, I hate to break it to you, but it's not!"

Dad opened his mouth, but no words came out. Freddy and Herb were staring at their sister like she'd suddenly grown an extra ear, right in the middle of her forehead.

Lucy heaved a sigh, and all the words she'd been holding back for far too long spilled out of her. "Nothing has been the same since Mom died. It makes me sick that we're pretending to have this big adventure in her honor, since she would absolutely *hate* the way you're sucking the fun out of it!" She stood up and put her hands on her hips. "You're spending this summer experimenting with the wrong thing, Dad. We've been wasting all this energy trying to get a stupid food truck up and running, but isn't it more important that our *family* work first? We're breaking down!"

Her dad gaped at her. Her siblings' mouths hung open. Lucy knew why: it wasn't like her to lose her cool. She was usually tough, hard, and unsmooshable. But today she was hot and frustrated, and she just wanted to flop down in a hammock and read her book. Or better yet, do nothing at all!

She was exhausted. And she missed her mom. She missed the way things used to be. If Mom were still alive, she would say: "Let's go grab an ice cream cone and find a lake to cool off in," or "Who's up for a little

Frisbee golf?" or even, "Great work today, kids, it's fun doing this as a team." But Dad didn't say any of that. He *never* said any of that.

Lucy quietly went on, "I wish you'd take a second to look at the big picture, instead of getting all bogged down in the stupid details of this so-called *Great* Peach Experiment. We're your *family*; not an *experiment*. The point of this summer shouldn't just be winning! This is my life, our summer *break*, and I hate that you're messing with it. I just want everything to go back to the way it used to be."

"Lucy . . . ," Dad began, his voice soft. There was a very long pause, during which his mouth opened, closed, and then finally opened again. "I'm trying."

"Are you really?" Lucy huffed, her hands on her hips.

"But, Lulu," Dad went on, slowly, as though he couldn't quite pull the words out of his brain. "We can never go back to exactly the way life used to be. I don't like it any more than you do, but that's reality."

Lucy felt hot, messy tears crowding into the space behind her eyeballs. She refused to let them spill. Then Herb scooted over and wrapped his arms around her tightly. He gave her a sad smile and rubbed his cheek against hers, and suddenly, she couldn't stop her tears from falling. Dad was right: nothing would ever be the same again. She had known this for a long time, but she'd refused to see it. She'd been trying so hard to cling to the life they'd once had, but it was time to figure out how to build a new family—just the four of them.

The time had come to let go of what *was*, and accept what *is*. She swiped at her face and said, "If this is how it's going to be, we need to make some changes."

Dad drew in a sharp breath. He looked at her, *really* looked at her in a way he hadn't in a long time. Then he closed his eyes, shook his head, and said nothing.

The kids all waited. The only sounds were the loud squeal and thunk of the campground's bathroom door in the distance, the trilling of chickadees in a tree over-head, and the pop of gravel as a car drove slowly past their campsite.

Lucy was the first to speak, after a long silence. "There *need* to be changes, Dad. We don't have a choice."

He glanced up at her. His eyes were unfocused, as though he'd drifted off into his own world—again. But then, finally, he said, "You're right."

"I am?" Lucy gasped.

"She is?" Herb asked.

"We can't go to Indianapolis," Dad said, dropping his chin into his hands. "I can't do it."

"Did we lose our permit?" Freddy asked.

"We need a break." Dad stood up. "I've been trying so hard to create a fun adventure for us. I just wanted to succeed at something, to show that we have what it takes—just the four of us—to function as a family. But simply chasing Mom's old dreams isn't the thing that's going to bring us together. Lucy's right: this isn't the solution." He looked at each of them in turn. "I don't want to let you kids down by giving up on our goal, but I seriously think we need to come up with a new plan."

Lucy cringed. She waited, wondering what "new plan" her dad would spout out next. At least chasing Mom's dream involved some element of whimsy and fun. Dad seemed to have lost his ability to have fun.

"What do you say we hit the road?" Dad said after a long pause. "Bail on the Peach Pie Truck and have some fun—a new way."

"What about the Food Truck Festival?" Freddy asked. "What about winning? We can't just *quit*. You said you don't like to fail, Dad? Well, I don't quit. *Mom* wouldn't quit. We've put in all this work, and I'm not going to let us give up completely."

"We can come back for the festival, if that's what we all decide we want to do," Dad said, nodding. "But we have a week before it starts, and a little more fun money to burn, so why not make the most of it? Another week of hard work and practice isn't going to make or break us at the festival. I haven't been to the beach in North

Carolina since I was a kid. We're halfway there. Let's pack up our stuff and go."

"To North Carolina?" Lucy asked. "To *the beach*?"

"To North Carolina!" Dad cried. Then he galloped around the table, waving his hat in the air like a full-on fool.

From the Sketchbook of Freddy Peach:
CRAZY CORN

We didn't stop a lot on the way from Ohio to North Carolina (it's a LONG drive), but we did see a couple cool things. There's this field in Dublin, Ohio, that is jam-packed with more than 100 giant cement corncobs. They're each more than six feet tall.

And how's THIS for odd? On the way through West Virginia, Dad surprised me by stopping in a town called Odd! That's the name: ODD! I'm pretty sure we almost careened off the road a few times on the way there, since Dad had to navigate the food truck through these narrow, winding mountain passes. It was SUPER beautiful, but also SUPER terrifying.

23

PEACH ON THE BEACH

The Peaches arrived in North Carolina very late, nearly midnight. They set up their tents in a small, rugged campground a few miles from Carolina Beach.

The next morning, when Lucy came back to their site from the campground bathroom, she found her dad packing up the truck. He looked like he was preparing to hit the road again. Lucy had known this change in plans had to be too good to be true, and now, it seemed, she'd been right again. "Are we leaving?" she asked.

"Yep," her dad said, securing all their food inside cabinets, the way they had to do before they drove anywhere. "We've got big plans, kid."

Lucy nodded, resigned to the fact that her father was simply incapable of doing nothing. It was obviously time for her to just accept who he was and adapt. "Where to now?"

Dad winked at her. Lucy took a step back. She had never, in all her life, seen her dad wink. To be honest, it was more of a squinty-blink, but she was pretty sure he'd been going for an actual *wink*. "To our beach house."

Lucy's eyebrows shot up. "Beach house?"

"Yep."

"For real?"

"I'm tired of living out of this truck and tents," Dad said. "We have some of Mom's fun money left over, and you've all been working really hard. We deserve to splurge a little. So I found a nice house that's available to rent for the next few nights. It's nothing fancy, but it's right on Kure Beach. That's not too far from here. It's near the spot I used to stay with my cousins, Aunt Lucinda, and Uncle Martin when I was a kid."

Lucy stepped forward and wrapped her dad in a huge hug.

"I hope that's okay?" Dad asked, his voice teasing. "Think Mom would mind me using a little of her invention money to spend a few days relaxing with you kids?"

"I don't think she'd mind at all," Lucy said. As she hugged her dad tight, she felt something inside herself unravel for the first time since their mom had died. "In fact, I'm pretty sure this would make her *very* happy."

🍮 🍮 🍮

A few hours later, they pulled up to a two-story house on stilts that was painted a crazy teal color. They parked the food truck in the driveway at the back of the house, then made their way around the side to a wooden staircase that led up to the door.

Inside, the house was bright and airy, and there were enough bedrooms that everyone got their very own space. It was Lucy's own little slice of heaven. "So, what's the plan for today?" she asked, after she'd unloaded her things into the neat little chest of drawers in her borrowed bedroom.

"Nothing," Dad said.

"Nothing?" Lucy repeated.

"I have *nothing* planned and *that's* the plan," Dad repeated. "I figure we can walk down to the beach, test out the waves, and then figure out what sounds good for dinner later."

As far as Lucy was concerned, this no-plan plan was too good to be true. She'd never been much of a do-nothing kind of girl, but at the moment, a few days of doing nothing sounded perfect. She still had fourteen books left to read on the seventh-grade summer reading list, and she was hoping she might have some time to sink into a few of them here at the beach. But if she didn't finish them all before the trip was over, she had decided that was totally okay, too.

"Beach time!" Herb screamed, tugging his swimsuit up over his buns as he raced into the living room.

Lucy began to load up a bag with sunscreen and snacks, but her dad gently set his hand on her arm. "I'm on it," he told her. She started to protest, then saw that her dad already had a bag filled with sunscreen, water bottles, a container of pretzels, and a few issues of his favorite journals: *Nature* and the very-boring-sounding *Earth and Planetary Science Letters*. He squeezed her shoulder. "I hope *you* know that *I* know how lucky Herb and Freddy are to have you for a sister. And I'm lucky you're my daughter. You've really stepped up and grown up these past few years, Lucy. I know it hasn't been easy, and I appreciate it."

She nodded. Until Dad said it, she hadn't realized that was just what she needed to hear. "Thank you."

"Thank *you*," Dad said with a smile. Then he called out, "Ready when you are, Herb-o. Freddy, you all set?"

Freddy hollered, "Coming!"

"Ocean, here we come!" whooped Herb.

Dear Great Aunt Lucinda,

Guess what?! Dad went totally crazy and abandoned ship (truck?)—but in a good way! We bailed on the next week of pie selling and set off on an epic family road trip to the BEACH instead. We've been boogie boarding and playing in the sand and reading in big chairs on our very own deck that overlooks the ocean! I can't believe I'm saying this, but now I wish there was more time left in the Great Peach Experiment, because I'm having SO MUCH FUN!!!

See you soon!

Lucy

(Give the dogs a big hug and an extra slice of bacon for me!)

24

CHANGE IN PLANS

On Monday morning, Freddy woke up early. He had left his window open, just a crack, the night before so he could hear ocean waves all night long. He was afraid if he couldn't hear it, none of this would turn out to be real. He lay in bed for a few long moments, listening to the gulls outside and thinking about some of the best parts of the past two days.

Kure Beach was amazing: wide and soft, and the waves were perfect—not too big, not too small. During their first afternoon at the beach, as the tide went out, all four Peaches had worked together to build a sandcastle village with a moat and towers that Herb had declared "the best sand-castle on earth." Then Freddy had spotted a pod of dolphins swimming by, right off shore by their house! Early Saturday evening, Dad had wandered down the road to a surf store and bought a few boogie boards. Then they spent all day Sunday trying to catch waves—as it turned out, boogie boarding was another thing Freddy excelled at. Maybe he didn't have *math* mastered, but at least he had a few solid backup plans. After they'd gotten tired of riding waves, they had built more sandcastles and played soccer on the beach. It had been one of the best weekends of Freddy's life.

After a bit of discussion during dinner the night before, the Peaches had all agreed they should spend the rest of the week doing a whole lot of nothing at the beach, and then they would head back to Ohio—rested and relaxed—in time for the Food Truck Festival. Freddy had been the one to propose this plan, and the others had been more than willing to go along with his idea. Freddy was excited they'd still get the chance to compete and try to succeed, but they'd also get some much-needed time together to practice being a new kind of family first. This plan brought together the best of both worlds.

Now, eager to get a start on another day of relaxing, Freddy padded down the hall of their rental house in his bare feet, heading toward the kitchen. He could hear his dad talking quietly on the phone. As he neared the big archway leading into the main dining area, he heard Dad say, "I can come back and figure it out. Just hold tight, and I'll be there as soon as possible." There was a short pause, then Dad went on, "There's a flight back to Minneapolis at four. If we hurry, I can catch it."

Freddy stopped short. He didn't like to eavesdrop, but his feet simply wouldn't move. He didn't know what he was hearing, but he knew he didn't like it. When he finally willed his legs to move, Freddy stepped through the archway into the kitchen and stared accusingly at Dad, who was staring down at his phone. "We're leaving?" he asked.

Lucy stumbled into the kitchen behind him, rubbing her eyes. "Who's leaving?"

"I got a call early this morning," Dad said. "They've found a massive error in some of our lab data, and a few of my graduate students need me to help them sort things out for an article that's due this week."

"Why do you need to go now?" Lucy asked. "Don't you study soil that's, like, thousands of years old? What's the big rush? You're supposed to be on sabbatical. You're taking a break from work, remember?"

"One of my colleagues is already at the lab, trying to weed through the data. Honestly, I don't know if there's much I can do," Dad said. "But I feel like I have to try. If I don't go back, the whole project will fall apart." He sighed. "This is everything I've been working toward for the past two years, Lucy. It's important."

Lucy muttered, "Obviously."

"And you have to leave *now*?" Freddy asked. His throat felt thick, the way it sometimes did when he was getting sick. "Can't we go back after the Ohio Food Truck Festival, at least?" He whispered, "This is important, too, right? We were going to spend the week hanging out together, and then finish with a bang selling a lot of pies. You promised we wouldn't just give up. Trust me, Dad, we could win the Food Truck Festival, and then—"

"They need me," Dad said, cutting him off.

"But *we* need you, too," Lucy said. Freddy had never, ever heard his sister say something like that. The look on Lucy's face made him feel even worse than he already did.

Dad sighed. "Look, we can figure out some way to get the food truck back to Ohio in time for the festival. Then we can fly down from Minneapolis and meet up with it there, if it's that important to you."

"It's not just the festival," Freddy said, shaking his head. But it was clear Dad wasn't planning to change his mind. He just didn't get it.

Lucy muttered, "I was stupid to ever let anyone get their hopes up." Then, with a huff, she turned and stormed out of the kitchen, leaving Freddy alone with Dad.

Freddy knew there was very little chance of Dad earning Lucy's forgiveness or trust—ever—if he chose to bail on them now. "Dad," Freddy said, trying to keep his tone even, "are you sure there isn't anyone else who can take care of this? You have a whole team that works with you at the university, and I just wonder if—"

Dad shook his head. "I need to be there. This is important."

"I know it is," Freddy said patiently. "I get that work is really important to you, and I think that's cool. I hope I love my job that much someday, too." He paused, trying to figure out how he could get Dad to change his mind. How he could convince him to pick *them* instead of *work*. How he could get him to see that they were important, too.

But in this moment, Dad was acting a lot like Lucy had at home for the past few years—trying to be the one who fixed everything, instead of trusting others to help when it made more sense. "This past month," Freddy began slowly, "our food truck has been the most successful when we all worked together, focusing on the stuff we're each best at, right? I'm great at customer service, Herb always has a positive attitude and handles the math, Lucy makes the best pies—"

Dad cut him off, glancing at the clock on the kitchen wall. "What's your point, Freddy?" He sighed. "I obviously don't have much of a choice here."

Freddy crossed his arms. "My point is, you're the one who told us the Great Peach Experiment was a *family* project. The goal of this summer was to experiment with something big, something Mom would have been proud to be a part of. You also told us, many times over the past few weeks, that we'd never succeed if we didn't all do our part." He shrugged. "You *do* have a choice, Dad. And I think you're making the wrong one. Ever since Mom died, you've *always* made the wrong decisions when it comes to us. But a few days ago, when we left Ohio, we all thought things were finally going to be different."

"I don't think you get it," Dad said. "This is the real world, Freddy. It's my life."

"So are we." Freddy shrugged. He'd made his point. Though he didn't want to, he knew when there was no other option but to give up and move on. So he turned and plodded back down the hall to Lucy's bedroom.

Propped up against the pillows in her big, cozy bed,

Lucy opened her arms and drew Freddy in beside her. A few minutes later, Herb joined them, and together, the three of them watched out the window as clusters of white, fluffy clouds gathered in the sky over the glittering, sapphire-blue ocean.

Freddy snuggled in with his siblings, thinking about how lucky it was that at least they had each other.

* * *

A few hours later, Dad came into Lucy's room, carrying a tray filled with glasses of lemonade and a bowl full of berries. Freddy and his siblings had done nothing to get ready to leave, and Dad hadn't asked them to. Freddy knew they would need to head to the airport very soon if they had any hope of making a four o'clock flight back to Minneapolis. "Hungry?" Dad asked, offering them all a small smile.

Lucy set down their tattered copy of *The Penderwicks*. They'd finally reached the last chapter, and Herb squirmed to show his frustration at having to put the book down.

Dad set the tray on the edge of the bed and settled in beside it. "I'm sorry," he said.

"For what?" Freddy asked.

"For even considering leaving, earlier this morning,"

Dad said. "For that, and for everything I've put you kids through the past few years. I've done a lot of thinking this morning, and I realize I owe you all a major apology."

Lucy folded the corner of the page and closed the book, refusing to look at their dad. She didn't say anything, but Freddy could tell she was listening.

"Lucy," Dad began, "you've been picking up my slack for far too long, and it's obvious that I have a lot to learn from you. I'm working on it. But I'm going to need your help figuring things out." He ran a hand through his thinning hair. "I'm grateful for everything you've done to step up and help manage this household the past couple years. Now, will you help me help you?"

Lucy nodded solemnly. "I'll try."

"That's all I ask," Dad said with a smile. "That's what I'm doing, too. I'm not always going to be perfect, but I promise to try to do my best."

Dad put his hand on Freddy's bare knee. "Freddy, I know how hard you've been working all summer to try to make sure this crazy, harebrained experiment of ours will succeed. You're so much like your mom, and it's been really exciting to watch you blossom, doing something you're obviously very skilled at. It's fun to see you in your element."

Freddy giggled and coughed at the same time. He couldn't help it. What his Dad had said was so *nice*, and it felt wonderful to get a compliment like that, but it was also so *goofy*. So a whole bunch of feelings just sort of bubbled up and out of him.

"I'm sorry I was prepared to walk out on this time together that matters so much to everyone," Dad said. "I want to make sure you all know that our family matters to me, too. More than anything. The past few weeks have been very special to me, and I don't want any of you to think otherwise. I know I don't always get my priorities straight, but I'm trying to fix that."

Next, Dad smoothed Herb's hair and said, "And you, Herbie: you've surprised me with how patient and optimistic and helpful you've been all summer. You took such good care of those mice, and you've proven time and again what a mature and capable kid you've become." Herb thrust out his chin proudly as Dad went on, "I'm sorry I haven't given you more chances to be an active part of this family. It's just hard for me to remember, sometimes, how big you've gotten."

"I wear a size three shoe now," Herb said in response. Then he plucked a berry out of the bowl and took a tiny sip of lemonade out of one of the tall glasses.

Dad laughed. "Good to know."

"So . . . ," Freddy said, scrunching his lips together, "you're staying?"

"I'm staying," Dad said.

"And you won't get fired or anything, because you're not going back to work?" Freddy clarified.

"I definitely won't get fired," Dad said, chuckling. "In fact, I think it's good for me to start to set some clear boundaries. My colleagues need to understand that my family comes first. Always."

"So we don't have to pack up and leave yet?" Freddy said, lifting his eyebrows.

"Not until we're good and ready," Dad said.

"Great. Now, while I have your attention," Freddy said, deciding that this was as good a time as any to bring up his latest idea. "I was thinking: if we do win the Ohio Food Truck Festival, what do you think about us splitting the winnings four ways? Even Steven—twenty-five hundred bucks a piece. So we can each decide what *we* want to do with our share."

Dad scratched his head and considered the question. "That seems fair."

"Then we'd better start doing some serious business planning," Freddy said. "Because we're gonna win."

HOW TO SPEND A MILLION DOLLARS

With a million bucks, I would buy a giant yacht and sail around the world with my family and friends. I'd even be okay with a houseboat that's just anchored somewhere breezy, like Kure Beach, in this amazing green-blue ocean water.

Actually, I'd be happy spending my million on exactly THIS, the adventure Dad took us on this week!

25

OPERATION HERBIE PEACH!

The first morning of the Food Truck Festival dawned clear and perfectly warm. The sky over Delaware, Ohio's old-fashioned main street was bright blue, the exact color of Herb's lucky marble (one of 227 marbles in his entire collection). The pink-and-yellow clouds stretching across the sky looked like gentle twists of cotton candy.

FOOD TRUCK FESTIVAL!

Less than an hour into the festival, Herb was already having a blast. He had been given a very important job for the weekend: he was now the official Peach Pie Truck mascot! For the next few days, his job was to wander up and down Delaware's main street—which looked like the movie set of a small town!—drawing attention to himself and his family's pie while dressed as a giant peach. Though the inflatable costume was hot, and it made his neck itch, Herb felt proud to be such an important part of the family business.

"You're cute and you're friendly," Freddy had explained when he presented the idea. "Who can say no to an adorable little kid dressed like peach?"

Though he didn't particularly like being called *little*, Herb quickly agreed to this plan. He was happy to do anything that would help his family succeed. Lucy did some investigating on Dad's phone and found a year-round Halloween shop in Columbus that was able to special-order a kid-sized inflatable peach costume.

Herb loved all the attention he got while he was dressed as a peach. Usually, he did not like when adults called him cute. But this was different. His head stuck out of a big, round, bright orange peach—and he knew he looked both silly and, yes, undoubtedly cute. "Well, aren't you just a peach?" one lady said, pulling out her cell phone to snap a picture of him. "Which truck are you from, sweetie?"

"We make world-famous pies at the Peach Pie

Truck!" Herb said, just like Freddy had coached him to do. Then, in a lower voice, he whispered, "Make sure you ask for an order of Herb's Cinnaballs on the side. . . . They're the yummiest."

Herb pranced up and down the sidewalks, smiling and waving and pointing people in the direction of the Peach Pie Truck. He held up a sign he'd made the night before, announcing their pie flavors (turtle pie was Herb's personal favorite, because it sounded more like a pet than pie):

Great Aunt Lucinda's Peach Pie
Apple Crumb Pie
Turtle Pie
World's Best Key Lime Pie

Key lime was a risky new addition to their menu. None of them had made this type of pie before, but the Peaches decided to include it in their festival menu after they went to a restaurant in Kure Beach whose sign boasted the "World's Best Key Lime Pie."

"I doubt that claim is true," Freddy had scoffed when he saw the sign. "They obviously haven't tried any of *our* pies yet." But after tasting it, each of them agreed that it was, quite possibly, one of the yummi-est things any of them had ever eaten. Even *Herb*, and he had started to actively *hate* pie. So before leaving North Carolina, the Peach family stopped to have lunch at that restaurant, and Freddy sweet-talked the chef into giving their family a lesson on how to make his "world's best" pie.

The filling was made using a fairly simple recipe. But even better, the pie called for a graham-cracker crust, which was made by angrily smashing graham crackers into tiny bits, then blending them with butter and pounding the whole mess into the bottom of a pan. This crust was so much easier to make than regular piecrusts, with all that fancy rolling and flopping and blind baking. Finally, Herb had found one type of crust even *he* could help make!

Heading into the festival, the Peaches had also made a few other changes. In order to have more space to spread out and bake *lots* of pies, Dad had rented space in something called a commissary kitchen. Herb learned that this was a special type of building that food trucks and catering companies could use when they needed extra space. Apparently, most food trucks used com-missary kitchens for food prep—these giant, shared kitchens made cooking a whole lot easier—but Dad had decided to work most of the summer out of their tiny food truck to keep costs low.

But now, for the first time all summer, the Peaches had a big, shiny kitchen to spread out in, and this allowed them to make more pies than Herb had ever seen in his life. In the two days leading up to the festival, they baked up a storm. Herb was finally allowed to help, and Freddy even let him use crust scraps make a few dozen orders of Herb's Cinnaballs to sell during the festival! By the time the competition started, the Peaches had dozens of gorgeous pies ready to sell.

In addition, Freddy had made a few adjustments to their business plan, hoping to help boost profits. That, Herb knew, meant they would make a lot more money without spending very much more money. They would still charge five dollars for a slice of pie, but customers could now add a scoop of ice cream for an additional two bucks. A big tub of ice cream cost only five dollars, and they could get at least twenty scoops out of each tub. Herb had done the math and realized this meant they would make thirty-five bucks per tub, give or take.

They didn't have a ton of freezer space in the food truck, so they could only keep three tubs of ice cream on hand. But Lucy had located the nearest grocery store, just two blocks from where their truck was stationed, and Herb had happily volunteered to be the designated ice cream runner whenever they needed to buy more. He was excited about his important new job.

After a long brainstorming session, they had also come up with a fun idea for how to offload any leftover pie in the afternoon. Dad had been the one to suggest that, starting at 3:14 every afternoon, they could offer a special deal: Pie for Pi. Before closing up shop, they would sell any remaining slices of pie for $3.14.

But with hours to go before closing time, Herb wanted to sell as much pie for full price as they possibly could. So while his family hung out in the hot and stuffy food truck, Herb trotted up and down the sidewalks, waving at possible customers and sneakily peeking into shops. He was very tempted to poke his head into the little antique shop to have a look around at all the treasures hidden inside, and there was a diner that looked super yummy. But he had a job to do, and Herb was committed. Finally, his family trusted him with something big, and he wasn't going to let them down.

He chatted with anyone who stopped to say hello, and carefully scoped out the competition. There were more than forty food trucks participating in the festival. Every truck had paid five hundred dollars to participate, and they were all gunning for the same ten-thousand-dollar prize. The food trucks were lined up from one end of the town all the way down to the Ohio Wesleyan University campus on the other end. Herb tried hard to remember everything he saw so he could report to his family. He wondered if anyone else wanted to earn that prize money as much as they did. Probably.

A few colorful trucks were selling tacos; one had a line, and Herb noticed that the people in that truck were all dancing and wearing fun hats. Another had fancy burgers, and the smells coming out of the truck were wonderful. Another truck had a sign advertising "Not Your Mama's Mac & Cheese," which Herb didn't understand, since his Mama had never *made* macaroni and cheese (his mom had made solar clings!). Several pastel-colored trucks had cakes and baked goods. One tall truck was painted to look like a giant ear of corn. There were Hawaiian meat-and-fruit skewers, massive turkey legs, smoothies, Italian street food, and even a cotton candy truck.

Lucy had packed a lunch for the family, so they wouldn't have to spend money at any of the compet-ing trucks—but Herb was so very tempted. The corn truck had a dancing ear of corn that spun around on top of their truck that made him instantly hungry. But he resisted! Instead, he wandered up to some of the people in the corn truck line, and said, "Hello, I'm Herb Peach and my family makes the yummiest pies! Right this way." He hopped from foot to foot, trying to get people's attention.

Sometimes, it worked. Other times, it did not.

But Herb liked to think the Peach Pie Truck had a long line of customers waiting for pie almost all day because of *his* efforts. Freddy seemed happy, which meant business was going well. And Herb had been asked to hustle off to the store several times to refill the food truck freezer with ice cream.

By the time three o'clock rolled around, they only had a few pies left to sell. As planned, they discounted their remaining treats to $3.14 per slice, and sold out of the remaining inventory just before four o'clock. As soon as they closed up shop, the Peaches celebrated. It had been a great day.

"I don't even need Herb to do his calculations to know we made a lot of money today," Freddy said. "We were busy! I'm pretty sure we made back all the money we spent on ingredients *and* our entry fee already."

"Can I get a *whoop whoop*?" Dad cheered.

Freddy made a funny face. "Um, no."

"One *whoop*?" Dad said.

"*Whoop!*" Herb hollered, running into Dad's arms.

Dad wrapped him in a hug, and Herb immediately heard a loud pop! Then something began to hiss. Herb glanced down and noticed that his inflatable peach costume suddenly looked less like a piece of *ripe* fruit and more like a piece of wilted, *dried* fruit.

"That was a *whoop* oops," Dad said, sheepishly holding up a pointy pie server. "It seems I accidentally popped our mascot."

26

THE FINAL SLICE

"Pie!" Freddy shouted from his perch at the food truck's service window the next morning. "Tasty pie! Who wants fresh-baked Peach family pie?"

The second day of the Food Truck Festival started out slow. Freddy could tell that some of the energy and excitement of the first day had dwindled, and there were much smaller crowds roaming up and down Delaware's main street. Still, he knew it was important that they keep up *their* energy and enthusiasm, since today, the judges would be going from truck to truck to do their scoring. They would be interviewing customers about each food truck's customer service, and secretly posing as customers to taste everyone's offerings. They would then combine that score with each truck's total profit for the festival in order to determine a winner.

So today, it was more important than ever to be at their very best and try to bring in even more sales. A few people wandered by, smiling politely, but very few people stopped to buy anything. "Maybe we could offer samples?" Lucy suggested.

"Can't hurt," Freddy agreed. "Remember Sample Stan, in Chicago?" he said, giggling. "*Everyone* loves samples."

So Freddy and Herb filled trays with small slivers of pie and headed out to chat with and tempt the passersby. Lucy and Dad stayed inside the truck to handle any customers who stopped to purchase.

Late that morning, Freddy also came up with another idea for bringing in business. "If not a lot of people feel like *eating* pie today," he told his family, "I'd be willing to sell a few slices that people could throw in my face if they want." He grinned. "Sales are sales, right?"

But fortunately, by midday, the Peach Pie Truck finally had a small line. Soon business was brisk, and they were selling slice after slice to eager customers. Freddy studied each person who came to the window, trying to figure out who the mystery judges were. It could be anyone: the lady with a stroller, the grumpy old man who had taken almost five minutes to pick his flavor of pie, the couple who asked if they ever sold pie by the *half* slice, the bearded twentysomething guy who refused to smile (but bought a slice of turtle pie and hurriedly gobbled it down).

"We're almost out of peach pie," Lucy announced shortly after lunch. "I sure hope the judges come by soon."

"Maybe they've already been here." Freddy shrugged. "Maybe it's this guy." A man in a checkered shirt and khaki slacks whisked his slice of peach pie off the counter and stepped away from the truck. Moments later, he fumbled for the beeping phone in his pocket. As he pulled it out, he lost his grip on the plate, and the entire slab of peach pie landed on the sidewalk with a messy *plop*!

The man fumed. "This pie—" he began, turning and shrieking at the Peaches. "This pie has *dirt* in it!"

"Uh, sir?" Freddy began politely. "I'm—"

Lucy blurted out, "You *dropped* your pie. That's why it has dirt in it."

"This pie is covered in dirt!" the man repeated. "I demand a refund."

The customers in line all stared at the unfolding action. Eager to diffuse the situation, Freddy thrust a five across the counter at him. Then he slid their very last slice of peach pie onto a fresh plate, along with a big scoop of ice cream. With a smile, he passed it to the man, and said, "Enjoy, okay? And I hope the rest of your day is just peachy."

All the other customers in line applauded. Dad and Lucy joined in. Freddy waved and grinned. Through his smile and gritted teeth, Freddy said to his family, "Let's hope that guy isn't a judge."

"But if he is," Dad said with a huge laugh, wrapping his arm around Freddy's shoulders, "thanks to your quick-thinking and good attitude, I think we may have just won."

🥧 🥧 🥧

The third and final day of the festival passed quickly. Sales were brisk at the Peach Pie Truck, but business was hopping at *all* the food trucks. It was impossible to predict who might win.

At five minutes to four, the Peaches were nearly sold out. They had just one pie remaining: a lone, ooey-gooey turtle pie. They had sold out of peach pie early in the day, because Herb had done an excellent job advertising that one, and Key lime pie had proven much more popular than any of them would have predicted.

"Well," Dad said, scanning the mess inside the food truck, "we done good."

"Yeah, we did," Freddy agreed. Everyone in the family had worked their butts off the past three days, and Freddy felt certain there was nothing more they could possibly have done to improve their outcome. "Even if we don't win, we certainly tried our hardest. I think Mom would be proud of us."

Dad nodded and pulled him in for a hug. "Son, I think you're right. I'd say we can officially call this experiment a success." He pulled back and studied Freddy's face carefully. "You know, you remind me more and more of your mother every day."

Freddy grinned. "Thanks."

Dad's face grew wistful, and a smile tugged at the corners of his mouth. "Your mom used to say, 'When inspiration strikes, you have to let it hit you—full force—and see where that jolt will take you.'" He chuckled. "I certainly think we lived up to that advice this summer."

"Speaking of stuff hitting you full force," Lucy said, kindly cutting into Freddy and Dad's awkward father-son moment. "It seems a shame to see this last pie go to waste. Remember Freddy's idea from yesterday morning?"

Freddy grinned. "You want to throw the last pie in my face!" he said, obviously delighted. "Don't you?"

But Lucy shook her head. "Nope," she said. "I want *you* to throw it in *my* face. I've always wanted to know what it would feel like to get pied." She grinned. "I have thirty dollars left from the fifty that Dad gave each of us to buy souvenirs this summer." She dug into her jean shorts pocket and pulled out a crumpled ten and four five-dollar bills. "I'm pretty sure this is the perfect way to spend the rest of my summer fun money."

Lucy hopped out the back door of the Peach Pie Truck and walked around to the service window, slapping her cash down on the counter. "Excuse me. I'd like to buy six full-price slices of turtle pie, please. No need to serve them up on plates; I'll take it in the pan, thanks."

Dad and Freddy exchanged a nervous look. This wasn't like Lucy. She wasn't usually a pie-in-the-face kind of girl. "Lucy," Dad began. "I'm not so—"

But before Dad could say no, Herb stepped up to the window and slid the gooey, whipped-cream-topped turtle pie across the counter to his sister. "If Lucy's willing to *pay* for this pie," Herb said, sounding like a little businessman, "we can't really tell her she can't have it. Money is money, and if Lucy buys the final pie, we'll be totally sold out. That's pretty cool."

Freddy shrugged. Herb had a point. Lucy could use her souvenir money however she wanted, and they could count this money toward their total earnings. If his crazy sister wanted to spend her own money to get pie-faced, he wasn't really in a position to tell her no.

So Freddy hopped out of the truck, grabbed the pie off the counter, and stood boldly in front of Lucy in the center of the sidewalk. He had always wanted to throw a pie in someone's face. "I have fifteen bucks left of my souvenir money," Freddy said, holding the pie high in the air. "Let's split the cost of this last pie, fifty-fifty, since this is going to be just as fun for me."

"Deal," Lucy said, laughing. Then she squeezed her eyes tight and said, "Hit me with your best shot."

Freddy pulled his arm back, then paused. "This was your idea, remember," he said. "I seriously hope there's not going to be payback for this." Then, before Lucy could change her mind, he yelled, "PEACH POWER!" and chucked the pie into his sister's face.

Ribbons of chocolate and caramel oozed down Lucy's shirt and pooled on her shoulders. She wiped whipped cream away from her eyes and squinted up at her brother. "Best use of souvenir money *ever*!" she declared.

"Agreed!" Freddy laughed and swiped a fingerful of whipped cream off his sister's cheek. "That image is going to stick with me forever."

☙ ☙ ☙

While Lucy got cleaned up, Freddy wiped down all the counters, Dad scrubbed dirty dishes in the sink, and Herb counted their money.

"If we subtract the five hundred dollars we spent to enter the competition, and our ingredient costs for the festival, we come out with three thousand three hundred and four dollars in total profits," Herb announced. "That's a lot of pie."

"Holy moly," Dad said. "I'd consider that a whopping success."

"Impressive," Lucy said, still swabbing sticky bits out of her hair.

"I knew we could do it," Freddy chimed in. Then he set off to turn in their final tally sheet at the judging booth.

Just as Freddy returned, a woman approached the Peach Pie Truck's service window. "Helloooo!" she called out, tapping on the counter.

"Sorry," Freddy called out cheerfully. "We're totally sold out of pie."

The lady came around to the back of the truck and poked her head through the big back door. "No worries, hon. I got a slice of that sweet peach pie earlier." She rubbed her belly. "Now I'm here on other business."

"How can we help you?" Freddy asked.

"My name's Lois Sibberson," the woman said. "I'm

getting everything set up to start a food truck of my own, and I'd be grateful if you'd let me take a quick peek inside your space."

"Absolutely," Freddy said. "What kind of truck are you opening?"

Ms. Sibberson smiled, and said, "I make pies, home-made bread, and scones that I've sold here at the Delaware farmer's market for years. I'm recently retired from my job as a fourth-grade teacher, and I've decided it's high time for me to set off on my next adventure. I've done a lot of research, and I'm ready to take my business on the road."

"It's hard work," Herb blurted out, his eyes wide. *"Really* hard work."

Ms. Sibberson laughed. "I know that. But I'm excited for the challenge. The only thing I have left to do is, I've got to find myself the right truck. I snuck a peek inside your vehicle when I ordered my pie earlier today and it seems to have a lot of the features I'm looking for in a truck of my own. If it's okay with you, I'd love to get a closer look inside to see if I can't get a few ideas."

Freddy glanced at Dad, who was staring at their guest with a strange look on his face. "So, Lois . . . ," Dad said slowly, "you haven't bought a truck yet?"

"Hoo, no!" Ms. Sibberson said, yelping with laughter.

"I was hoping to find a used truck, so I don't have to build the whole thing from scratch. But used food trucks aren't an easy thing to come by here in the middle of Ohio."

Lucy and Herb hopped out of the truck to give Ms. Sibberson some space. Using Freddy's arm for support, Ms. Sibberson stepped up into the Peach Pie Truck. She looked around, nodding appreciatively. "Yep, this is just the sort of food truck I've been searching for. Would be fun to have some extra seats up front for my grandkids to join me on my travels sometimes." She laughed, then added, "Don't suppose you want to sell, do ya?"

Freddy looked at Dad, who stared back at him, his eyebrows raised in a question. "Fred?" Dad asked. Freddy felt himself flush with pride—his dad had turned to *him* for advice. He took a deep breath. He didn't even need to ask his siblings their opinion; he was pretty sure they would all agree with his assessment: this experiment had officially run its course.

Freddy was one-hundred-percent certain they were not cut out to be a food truck family. It had been a fun experiment, but it was time for them to move on to their next adventure. Freddy gave his dad a brief nod, and Dad responded with a slight nod of his own. Lucy and Herb nodded their agreement, too.

"Lois," Freddy said seriously, "let's make a deal."

※ ※ ※

Just as they finalized their deal with Ms. Sibberson—who was willing and able to pay the Peaches the *exact* amount Dad had spent on the truck in the first place—the festival organizers announced that they were ready to reveal the results.

"In fourth place"—the Peaches all linked arms, bracing themselves for the announcement—"with solid marks for flavor and service, and a total three-day profit of one thousand nine hundred thirty-six dollars: Corn Cabin!" There was a smattering of applause from the big corn-shaped truck.

"In third place, also with a near-perfect score for service and flavor"—Freddy squeezed his eyes closed—"and a total three-day profit of two thousand two hundred ninety-two dollars: Taco Cat!"

"Our runners-up, with excellent marks for flavor, and a total profit of three thousand two hundred eighty-two: the Burger Boys! Congratulations!" A loud roar came from the Burger Boys at the other end of Delaware's main street.

"And now, the winner of the Ohio Food Truck Festival and the ten-thousand-dollar grand prize. With *perfect* marks for taste and service and a total profit of three thousand three hundred and four dollars—bringing in just twenty-two dollars more than the Burger Boys—the Peach Pie Truck."

"We did it!" Freddy screamed, overcome with emotion. "We *won!*"

The Peach family cheered and jumped up and down and even joined Dad in a few little *Whoop whoop*s! All four of them squeezed into a giant hug and jumped up and down some more.

"We won," Lucy echoed, as she lifted Herb into the air. Herb blew kisses at all the people cheering for them. "By just twenty-two bucks. Wow."

"Yes!" Dad tossed his hat into the air and pumped his fist. "Good thing my smart kids bought that last turtle pie, or we would have come in second!"

Freddy set off to collect their prize check and certificate from the festival organizers, taking a few extra minutes to shake hands with all the judges on behalf of the family. "Thank you," he told them. "It's an honor." Then he turned and bowed, accepting congratulations and pats on the back from random people in the crowd.

"So . . . was it worth it?" Dad asked the kids a few minutes later as they strolled together down the main street to offer congratulations to the Burger

Boys, Taco Cat, and Corn Cabin. "Are you glad we did this?"

Freddy smiled at him. "Of *course* it was worth it." Even though there had been plenty of challenges along the way, and even if sometimes it had been tempting to give up, and even though they had spent much of the past month stuffed inside an overly hot, cramped, and messy food truck, there was no doubt about it: this had been a crazy adventure to remember. Their summer experiment hadn't gone exactly as planned, but it had *definitely* been worth it.

From now on, Freddy was committed to following Mom's best advice: he would make sure his family tried to make the most out of life, even when the going got rough. *When life gives you lemons, make peach pie.* He smiled as he thought about his family's new version of Mom's favorite phrase.

Though they'd had a rough couple of years, and though it would certainly take time and a lot more false starts and do-overs, Freddy was certain that eventually the Peaches would be pretty incredible again.

27

CHANGING LUCK

After nearly a month on the road, Lucy was ready to head home. As soon as the Food Truck Festival wrapped up, the Peaches bid Lois Sibberson and their food truck farewell, rented a car to get back to Minnesota, and headed to their last campground for one final night in their tents. After stopping to take a quick swim in Delaware's community pool to cool off, they packed everything up so they could hit the road first thing the next morning.

It was a long drive back to Duluth—more than twelve hours. Even though it was a relief to finally have a vehicle with air-conditioning, neither of the boys was looking forward to spending a whole day in their rental car. Lucy was exhausted, but she was excited to finally get some more dedicated reading time. She hadn't read at all during the Food Truck Festival, and she was more than ready to get back to the last dozen or so books on her summer reading list.

But after a couple quiet hours on the road, Lucy's book slipped out of her hands and she fell fast asleep. She was startled awake a few hours later when Dad pulled off the highway to get gas. Her brothers had both been sound asleep, too—Freddy had a crusty line of drool that looked like a tree branch on his left cheek, and Herb was dozing so deeply that he had to be shaken awake.

Inside the gas station, they all hit the bathroom, and then Lucy hung out with Herb while he scanned the rows of colorful lottery tickets lining the counter near the cashier. When Dad came out of the restroom, Herb pointed at the tempting line of scratch-off tickets hidden behind clear glass. "Please?" he begged. "Just one? For all of us to share?"

Dad sighed and shook his head. "Lottery tickets aren't for kids, Herb."

Herb nodded sadly, then perked up the tiniest bit. "Even if I use my own money? I have two dollars of my souvenir money left—you said I could spend it on whatever I want. This is what I want."

"We've discussed this." Dad said. "Lottery tickets are a waste of money, not a game."

Lucy and Herb were almost to the door when Dad called out, "But I guess one can't hurt. This whole trip has been a big gamble, right? A gamble that ultimately paid off." Lucy turned just in time to see Dad pull two crumpled one-dollar bills out of his pocket and hand them over to the cashier.

"Let's save it for when we get home," Lucy suggested to Herb. "It will give you something to look forward to." Herb had been waiting all month long for their dad to splurge on a lottery ticket—she trusted that he could wait a little while longer to scratch it off. So she let him take the ticket, and Herb stuffed it into his pocket, nodding solemnly.

The Peaches piled back into their rental car and buckled up. But when they pulled out of the gas station lot, Dad didn't turn left to follow signs toward the highway home. He turned right, following a long, winding road past sandwich shops and more gas stations. "You took a wrong turn," Lucy told him.

"Did I?" Dad asked.

"The highway is thataway," Herb announced from the back seat.

"Well, maybe we should just see what's down here," Dad said. "I think there might be an interesting roadside attraction down this way, and we have Freddy's summer goal to keep in mind." He peered into the rear-view mirror and attempted a wink. Moments later, he eased the car into a narrow space on the far end of a giant parking lot.

"Why are we stopping again?" Freddy yawned, covering his face with his sweatshirt.

"I'm a little tired of driving," Dad said in a funny voice.

The kids all exchanged confused looks.

"Maybe we should just stop here for the night?" Dad suggested.

"Where *are* we?" Herb asked, peering out the window.

Lucy guessed there were hundreds—maybe thousands—of cars parked all around them. It was like a car zoo.

"Wisconsin Dells," Dad said simply. "Waterpark Capital of the World."

Lucy watched Herb's face light up at the promise of waterslides and pools galore. But then his expression grew dark again. "You're joking."

"That's not funny, Dad," Lucy said.

"I'm actually very serious," Dad said. "I took part of my Food Truck Festival winnings and booked us a room at a water park hotel tonight. I thought we could finish our drive tomorrow, and spend the rest of this afternoon riding waterslides instead? After all, I did promise Herb he could go swimming every day, and we have a few dry days to make up for. Hopefully this will do the trick?"

There was a momentary pause, then all three Peach kids screamed at once.

Dad covered his ears. "I'm going to take that as a yes."

🍑 🍑 🍑

That night, after they'd spent hours going down water-slides and drinking more fruit smoothies by the pool than anyone was willing to admit, the Peaches went out for pizza at one of the hotel's many theme restaurants. A friendly waiter set a gleaming silver pan atop a giant can of stewed tomatoes, and everyone slid a gooey slice of pizza onto their plates.

While Herb waited for his pizza to cool, he reached into his shorts pocket and pulled out the lottery ticket Dad had bought for them earlier that afternoon. "I almost forgot!" he said. "We were going to wait to scratch this until we got home. But since we're not *going* home yet, maybe we could just do it here instead?"

"Why not?" Dad said with a shrug. He read the lottery ticket instructions aloud: "To win, you must match the symbol in one of the picnic baskets to the winning symbol shown in the prize box."

Dad pulled a coin out of his pocket and scratched the foil off the "prize" box. "The winning symbol is a pie!" he announced, obviously delighted.

"That's serendipity!" Herb declared.

Next, Freddy scratched the silver foil off one of the picnic baskets. "I got a stupid fish," he said. "Not a winner."

One by one, each Peach took turns scratching another box on the ticket. "I got a flower," Lucy announced.

"A campfire," Dad groaned.

"I got a hot dog," Herb said. He pushed the ticket into the center of the table. "There's one picnic basket left to open. Who wants to scratch it?"

"Let's call this one Mom's box," Lucy suggested. "Maybe she'll have more luck than the rest of us did. You can scratch it for her, Herb."

"For Mom," Herb said seriously. Then he pursed his lips together and scratched off the last bits of silver. "It's a pie!" he shrieked. "We won two dollars!"

They all cheered, celebrating almost as vigorously as they had after winning the Ohio Food Truck Festival. Then Herb stood up on the seat in their booth and kissed the winning lottery ticket. "I love you, I love you, I *love* you!"

"You know, I'm starting to think our luck might be changing," Dad said, laughing. "We've got good stuff on the horizon."

"I think you're right," Lucy said. Though they weren't anywhere near perfect, and it was obviously going to take a long time for them to patch up all the cracks in their fractured family, Lucy finally felt like they were making progress. And even more important, she was starting to trust that their dad might eventually figure out how to lead their family in his own kind of way. For the very first time since their mom had died, Lucy was proud to be a Peach.

"It's not luck," Freddy said, pounding the table so hard the plates rattled. "It's Peach power!"

"Peach power!" Dad and Herb repeated, pumping their fists.

Then they all looked at Lucy, eyebrows lifted

expectantly. As Herb tackled her into a huge hug, Lucy laughed and shrieked, "Peach power!" In that moment, Lucy felt something she hadn't in a long while: she felt like part of a complete family. A sweet, perfectly messy peach pie of a family.

My dearest Lucy and family,

Welcome home! I have some news. After living in this giant house for the past fifty years (with only the dogs to keep me company for the last ten of them!), I've decided the time has come for me to find a home more suitable to a single woman of my age. I've rented an apartment in the same "old folks" complex where my best friend lives. (Lucky for me, the facility is also <u>filled</u> with card players, so I can play Hearts all day and night, if I so choose!)

I can't stomach the idea of someone outside the family taking over this wonderful old mansion and moving into my family's home. Because the four of you are the only family I have remaining in Duluth— and because your mother always told me she dreamed of one day living here (and possibly turning the extra rooms into a bed-and-breakfast?!)—I've decided it makes sense to pass the house on to your father to enjoy with you three kids.

The place needs work—a lot of work. Frankly, it's become a bit of a pit, since I really only spend time on the main floor these days. And the dogs will have to stay put. My new apartment doesn't allow animals, and these hairy little wig-stealing beasts need more entertainment and attention than this old lady can provide.

But after reading all the postcards you sent during your family's great summer adventure, I think you're up to the task and the challenge. Please come by the house to talk further about the next Great Peach Experiment just as soon as you've unpacked from your travels. . . .

Much love, Your
Great Aunt Lucinda

AUTHOR'S NOTE

Please be aware that I took *significant* liberties with the actual laws, permits, regulations, and day-to-day operations of a food truck. Of course, I did extensive research into this type of business venture and used real laws to help guide my writing, but I also chose to ignore or change some of the information I found. For the sake of a fun story, I made a lot of things up (and exaggerated or ignored some facts) along the way.

If you ever consider starting up a food truck, *please* do more research and planning than the Peach family did. This book is a work of fiction, and in the real world, this business would have taken much longer to get off the ground, and a start-up like this likely would have fared much, *much* worse in real life.

The best part of writing fiction is, you get to make stuff up. So I did just that. And I certainly hope you enjoyed the adventure.

🥟 🥟 🥟

Writing a great book, like many of life's best adventures, requires the assistance, company, and support of many other people. The first draft of this story came together really quickly, but the revisions and recipe refinement for the Peach family's adventures took years. My editor (and great friend!) Bethany Buck deserves a lifetime supply of perfect pie for her spot-on advice, encouragement, and editorial direction for this story.

My agent, Michael Bourret, has been with me for the long haul on this publishing journey, and always keeps me from taking a wrong turn, even when the going gets rough and I've clearly lost my way.

My family—Greg, Milla, Henry, Ruby, and my snuggly pup, Wally—inspired many of the events and adventures in this story and make life perfectly peachy every single day. My talented son, Henry, drew all of Freddy's art for this book, Ruby helped me write Lucy's letters, and all three of my kids came up with the unique Blues Festival beards and helped me develop many of the best plot twists in the story. Your creativity and cleverness astound me, kids; may the three of you always be so funny and cheerful and clever.

My mom—Barb Soderberg—read at *least* twenty drafts of this story and helped out in some way at every stage. My dad—Kurt Soderberg—helpfully read a few drafts, too, and pointed out some of the things that were too weird, even for him (truth be told, there's not much that's *too* weird or quirky for me and my dad!).

I couldn't survive this sometimes-lonely job without my crew of writer friends—Cathy Clark, Anica Rissi, Robin Wasserman, Laura Zimmermann, my fellow Renegades of Middle Grade, and many others—who read drafts, brainstorm, commiserate, and cheer me on.

A few real-world places and people unknowingly helped out with this story, and I'd like to say thanks: to Mike Lowery (whose magnificent and fun random facts books helped inspire that slice of Freddy's character); to the real-world Betty's Pies and my late Grandma Wilma (for making me a pie-lover); to the Sasquatch Food Truck (for letting me roam around and investigate your truck, as well as for answering a bunch of food truck–operating questions while you whipped up my yummy order).

Many teacher friends have supported and encouraged me over the years by sharing my books with their students, inviting me for school visits, and passing along tons of recommendations for books I would enjoy reading—Melissa, Lesley, Kristen, Jason, Michele, Julie, Sandy, Kurt, Carrie, Beth, Pam, Jennifer, Niki, Laura, John, Susan, Franki, Katie, and so many more. I can't possibly thank you all individually—and I know some of you don't like to be mentioned by name in the back of a book—so just know that I'm thinking of you, too! I do, however, want to express special recognition to the four teachers who invited me into their classrooms as part of the #KidsNeedMentors program the past few years. So, thanks to Tracey Maniotis, Kristen Loiacono, Leigh Ann Salas, and Vi Figueroa for the friendship and writing connection with your bright and inquisitive students. Also, a shout-out to my teacher friend Patrick Andrus, who has brought me into his classroom every year for his breakfast book club and has shared and discussed early drafts of many of my novels with his students.

Huge thanks to my publishing partners at Pixel+Ink —including brilliant copyeditor Susan Wilkins, Raina Putter, Lisa Lee, Terry Borzumato-Greenberg, Michelle Montague, Cheryl Lew, Nicole Benevento, Emily Mannon, Miriam Miller, Julia Gallagher, Adrienne Vaughan, Derek Stordahl, Andy Ball, Hannah Fine, Jessica Dartnell, Alison Weiss, and Kyra Reppen. Also the Penguin Random House sales and distribution team. Finally, a word about this book's talented designer, Michelle Cunningham: your design is like the ice cream on top of a warm slice of apple pie—you really took this book to the next level and made it shine. It's been such a delight going on this journey with all of you, and I look forward to our next great adventure.